"Ferry blends a nostalgic tone of yesteryear with a discerning portrayal of a girl struggling toward understanding her parents, grappling with changes wrought by the war and graduation, and searching for her own place."
Booklist

"Charles Ferry has capably made his point about the young person of 1944 and his 1977 counterpart: in the fundamentals, nothing has changed."
Best Sellers

"A gently written period piece, with authentic small town and Midwest atmosphere."
University of Minnesota

O
Zebron
Falls!

This is a revised edition. The story is unchanged, but the author has done minor editing to the main text and condensed the final scene of the book.

The fictional town of Zebron Falls is actually the village of Rochester, Michigan, as it was in the 1940s.

Charles Ferry has been a resident of the Rochester area for 36 years.

You will notice some vulgar language in reference to race in this book. The original wording has not been altered, inasmuch as it is a historical reflection of the period. No offense was intended in the original edition; none is intended now.

O Zebron Falls!

CHARLES FERRY

Proctor Publications
Ann Arbor, Michigan 1994

Publisher's Cataloging Recommendations:

Ferry, Charles, 1927—
O Zebron Falls!

  SUMMARY: an unresolved conflict with her
father, imminent high school graduation, and World
War II complicate a young girl's struggle to
shape her life.

  1. Title.
  2. World War II, homefront.
Library of Congress Catalog Card Number 94-67373
ISBN 1-882792-04-1

To the memory of
my mother and my father.

Also by
CHARLES FERRY

Binge
(Proctor Publications 1992)

One More Time!
(Houghton Mifflin 1985)

Raspberry One
(Houghton Mifflin 1983)

Up in Sister Bay
(Houghton Mifflin 1975)

O
Zebron
Falls!

Part One

Part One

1

Lukie Bishop hurried to get home — up Wilcox Street and through the cemetery, following her private path around the headstones and the flagpole and the weathered statue of Joshua Zebron. It was raining, a cold, pelting autumn rain.

She would go over to Great Oaks after supper, she decided, and thank Billy. The Student Council vote had been unanimous, Mr. Panella had told her, but she was sure Billy had fixed it for her. He knew how badly she had wanted the appointment, that her plan for her father and her Uncle Farnie depended on it — and Billy could fix anything.

She came out of the cemetery and turned up Old Perch Road, past the waterworks and the village limits, walking on her toes to avoid the puddles in the gravel surface of the road — a slender, leggy girl in a red plaid skirt and a yellow slicker. The wind blew in the trees. Smoke trailed up from the chimneys. The rain stung her cheeks and gave the fallen leaves a rich, earthy smell. Lukie loved autumn. Autumn was a lovely settling-in, and it made you want to do things.

She debated whether she should talk to her father when he got home from the mill. No, he might be in a bad mood. It would be better to work on Uncle Farnie first, to use him as a wedge. Her father would require — tact.

The Bishop place was near the end of Old Perch Road. Tall shade trees lined the driveway, and bittersweet vines grew wild in the fence along the road. As the gabled roof came into view through the trees, she broke into a run, one arm clutching her books and the other holding down her skirt in the wind. Her dog, Lady, an aging German shepherd, came barking down the lawn to greet her.

"I'm homecoming chairman, Lady!" Lukie bent over and let the dog lick her face. "Isn't that keen?"

And then leaping up the porch steps, and bursting into the house, and letting her books clatter onto the little table in the front hall —

"Mama, Mama, I'm homecoming chairman!"

"Of course you are, dear," a voice called back. "Did you think for a minute they would choose anyone else?"

Myrene Bishop, a small, erect woman with cheerful eyes and a bright imperturbable manner, was at her easel in the sunroom — attired in a flannel skirt and one of her husband's old wool hunting shirts, which she used as a smock when painting. Of the three Bishop children, Beth and Buddy strongly favored their father, but even

4

strangers knew at a glance that Lukie was her mother's daughter.

"Oh, Mama, I feel so scared!" Lukie gave her mother a quick kiss and then collapsed on the wicker footstool next to the easel, out of breath. "I'll be in charge of every-thing — the parade and the rally and the dance."

"Relax, dear," her mother said soothingly. "You'll do just fine. Who organized the debating tournament and the matinee dances?"

"I know, Mama." Lukie sighed. "But this is different. We're going to win the championship. The whole school will be depending on me."

"You'll do just fine, dear." Myrene Bishop smiled, pat-ting her daughter's hand. "You'll have Sally to help you — and Billy." She collected her brushes and dipped them in a little bowl of turpentine. "Now run upstairs and change. Your father will be home in a few minutes, and your feet are soaked."

"How come he's coming home so early?"

"He has to work late tonight. They're installing a new loom for the Army contract."

"Oh, honestly, Mama," Lukie complained, "why doesn't he just move into that dumb mill! We could send over his meals and forward his mail."

"There's a war on, dear, and your father has important responsibilities."

"But he's only the manager, Mama. It's not as if he owned the place."

"Your father kept that mill alive when half the town was dying," Myrene Bishop said quietly. "It's nothing to make light of, Miss Smarty Pants."

5

"I know." Lukie looked glum. "I'm sorry."

She got to her feet and shook out her damp skirt.

"Will you tell Daddy about my appointment, Mama?"

"Don't you want to tell him yourself?"

"I feel nervous when I talk to him about things at school. He makes me feel as if I'm bragging, or something."

"You shouldn't feel that way, dear. After all, he is your father."

"I know," Lukie said pensively. "But I do."

And then, with her dog still at her heels, through the dining room and into the kitchen, pausing briefly to peek at the pork roast that was browning in the oven, and then up the back stairway, which was also used as a pantry —

"Mama, tell Beth and Buddy not to pester me when they get home," she called back. "And, oh, darn! I haven't started on the storm windows yet, but please, Mama — oh, please, please, please! — don't let Daddy crab at me, tonight of all nights!"

Alone in her bedroom, having changed into jeans and a floppy sweater, and with Lady stretched out contentedly on the mat next to the bed, she brushed out her long black hair and then curled up in the dormer windowseat with her diary. The rain tapped pleasantly on the roof, and the wind blew in the eaves. The dormer window offered a beautiful view. Below the orchard and beyond a windbreak of Lombardy poplars, the south pasture of Great Oaks Farm sloped down toward the river; and to the east, the landmarks of the town rose high above the trees — the bell tower of the high school, and the church

6

spires, and the village water tower, with its faded legend:

ZEBRON FALLS

POP. 4216

They would have to paint the water tower, she thought — if they won. And if they lost? No, they wouldn't lose. Billy had promised, and Billy Butts never broke his word. Still, somebody had to lose.

She sat there for several minutes, gazing out the window and collecting her thoughts. Then she opened the diary and began to write.

September 28, 1942

Dear Diary,

I did it! Today I was named homecoming chairman, and afterward Harvey Toles came up and congratulated me. Sally thinks he might ask me to the dance, but he's so wrapped up in his music he hardly knows I'm alive. I'll probably end up with the wallflowers again —

Her writing was interrupted by the sound of footsteps out in the hall. She looked up and saw her father standing in the doorway — a tall, square-faced man in a shirt and a tie and the thin jacket he wore at the mill.

"Hello, Daddy," she said anxiously.

"Your mother says you haven't started on the storms yet." Walter Bishop frowned.

"It's raining."

"It's not raining out in the garage, is it?"

"But you can't wipe them clean when the air is humid."

Walter Bishop shook his head skeptically. "You're just full of excuses, aren't you?"

"It's not an excuse, Daddy," Lukie protested. "You have to rub your arm off to get the streaks out."

"Well — they'd better be spick-and-span by next Saturday. I'm going to start putting them up."

"Do you want me to hold the ladder?" Lukie offered.

"No," Walter Bishop said, glancing away from his daughter. "Buddy's going to help me."

He turned to leave.

"Daddy —" Lukie said.

"Yes?"

"I'm homecoming chairman."

"Yes." Her father nodded. "Your mother told me. Will it take up much of your time?"

"A little, I guess."

"Well, if it interferes with your studies you'll have to give it up. I'm expecting straight A's this semester."

When he had gone, Lukie stared emptily out the dormer window. He had ruined it. She wasn't sure what she had expected — a hug, a handshake, *some*thing. It was just his nature, her mother had explained; it embarrassed him to show his feelings. Maybe. But he roughhoused with Buddy and twirled Beth in his arms, even though she was in eighth grade and big for her age. And she hadn't forgotten the business over her portrait. It had happened long ago, but she hadn't forgotten.

She sat at the window until it began to grow dark. Then she slipped down the back stairway and out of the house and walked down through the orchard to the river. The river would help, she thought. The river always helped.

2

The Bishop place had once been a dairy farm, but during the Depression the fields and pastures had been sold off to Great Oaks to help the family survive. Now, all that remained of the farm was the broken foundation of a silo and a neglected apple orchard, which ran from Lukie's vegetable garden down to the river. Above the orchard, where the shoreline of the river rose in wooded bluffs, was Lukie's secret retreat — a little hollow in the face of a hill, sheltered on three sides by jack pines but open to the river. She often went there when she felt troubled or confused — or when her father crabbed at her. Buddy, her little brother, knew she had a secret spot, but he had never managed to track her there. He kept pestering her to bequeath the spot to him. It was dumb for a grown girl to have a hideout, he'd complain, and besides, he needed it for a fort. But Lukie wasn't ready to give it up — not yet.

Lukie's bedroom was in the rear of the house, above the kitchen. It had belonged to her Uncle Farnie, and still contained mementos of his youth — the forgotten high school yearbook in the bookcase, the initials inscribed in the base of the gooseneck lamp on the desk, the knapsack in the closet with his things from the war — his mess kit, his gas mask, his leather aviator's helmet. Uncle Farnie and his twin brother, Lukie's father, had been heroes in the Great War, having shot down seven German Fokkers between them. And before that, they had been the famous "Buttermilk Twins" of the Zebron High football team, so named because one of their chores on the farm had been to cart the big galvanized milk cans to the depot before school every morning. Walter Bishop still had a speech impediment from having been shell-shocked at Château-Thierry — a slight stammer that showed when he got excited — and Uncle Farnie had been in a veterans' hospital for nearly a year after the Armistice, although nobody seemed to know the exact nature of his wounds.

It was hard for Lukie to imagine her father and Uncle Farnie having done such exciting things together, for they barely spoke to each other anymore. After the war, there had been a falling-out — over the settling of Grandpa Bishop's estate, her mother had told her, although Lukie had heard whispers that it went much deeper than just money. Whatever the reason, Uncle Farnie was never at the house for Lukie's birthday parties or for any of the big family gatherings, not even the night she was accepted into the Tuesday Musicale — until finally she despaired of ever having her uncle, who was her best friend, save for Billy Butts, share in the important occasions of her life.

But if Uncle Farnie never visited at the big house out on Old Perch Road, it was easy enough for Lukie to visit him — at Higbie Manufacturing, where he worked as a die-maker, or at his bachelor's quarters behind Rosemergy's place on Lysander Street, or at the tap room of the St. James Hotel. Uncle Farnie was a regular at the tap room, and on nights when he'd had a bit too much, Mr. Cromie, the bartender, would call the house and ask if Lukie would please come down and help her uncle home. These were delightful occasions for her — maneuvering Uncle Farnie out of the smoky tap room and across the carpeted hotel parlor, and then walking with him through the darkened town. Lukie was proud of being Uncle Farnie's niece. Uncle Farnie had a way about him. Sometimes she thought she loved him more than she loved her father — and felt guilty about thinking that way.

"Maybe that's why your dad crabs at you so much," Billy had suggested to her last summer. "Because you're so tight with your Uncle Farnie."

And it was that remark that had led to Lukie's plan to use the homecoming festivities as a device to force a reconciliation between the brothers. She would persuade the school to proclaim homecoming day "Buttermilk Twins Day." Mr. Seed, at the *Clarion*, would run a big article, and they would be the talk of the town. There would be a special float for them in the parade and a presentation at half time. They would talk of old times, and the hard feelings would wash away.

11

But when Lukie confided her plan to her mother, she received little encouragement.

"They're both very stubborn men, dear. Don't get your hopes up too high."

"But what *is* it with them, Mama?" Lukie asked impatiently. "I mean, the way Daddy clams up when anybody mentions Uncle Farnie, you'd think there's some dark family secret he's trying to cover up."

Myrene Bishop glanced reprovingly at Lukie.

"Don't pry, Lukie," she said shortly. "Every generation is entitled to its privacies."

And then, softening, she smiled and gave her daughter a little hug.

"I'll work on your father," she agreed. "Now, how would you like to have an open-house after the big game?"

And so September gave way to October. The deepening colors of autumn spread slowly over the little town in the valley. Pumpkins turned orange on the hillsides. The apple harvest commenced, and on Saturday afternoons the roar of the crowd echoed from Halbach Field, where Billy Butts was leading an inspired Zebron High football team to victory after victory.

With a little cooperation from the Buttermilk Twins, Lukie thought, it would be a fine homecoming.

3

They were in Assembly. Mr. Severence, the principal, had just finished introducing Billy Butts and Junior Rosenquist and the rest of the football team.

"Don't look now," Sally whispered to Lukie, "but Harvey Toles is staring at you."

Lukie and her friend Sally DeBaene were seated in the front row, for Lukie would be called on next to give a report on homecoming-week activities.

"Where's he sitting?" Lukie whispered back.

"To your right, four rows back."

Lukie started to turn around.

"Not so *ob*vious!" Sally hissed. "Turn your head *ca*sually."

Lukie pretended to have dropped something, and as she leaned forward she stole a glance over her shoulder. Harvey Toles *was* staring at her — or was he looking at

Sally, who was the prettiest girl in the junior class? She glanced back again. No, he was looking unmistakably at her. A warm flush came over her cheeks. She wished she'd worn her new angora sweater instead of her old corduroy jumper.

". . . and now," Mr. Severence was saying, "Lukie Bishop, our homecoming chairman, will give us a progress report."

Lukie hurried up to the stage at the end of the gymnasium, flustered. She tripped on the microphone cord, and her knees kept shaking.

"Mr. Eberline says it's all right for us to use his pasture up on South Hill for the bonfire, and Lorena Pearsall's father at the D and C will donate all the bunting and crepe paper we need."

She rushed through the notes she'd stayed up late preparing — about the floats, and the alumni reception, and Mr. Leiber's new victory song, which would be played at the game and also at the dance. The dance would have a Halloween theme, and there would be corn shocks and jack-o'-lanterns and soft lights that kept changing colors.

"There's only one problem," she concluded. "We couldn't locate a dance band that we could afford, but Mr. Knapp at the Sweet Shoppe is going to lend us his jukebox for the night, so at least we'll have all the latest songs."

When she had finished, she felt sure she'd made a fool of herself, but there was a big round of applause, and afterward Harvey Toles cornered her in the Main Hall. Lukie felt her heart racing.

"I don't know if you'd be interested," he said, "but I've

been organizing a six-piece band to play up at Ollie Trout's roadhouse next summer. If we can get ready in time, we'll play for the dance."

"Oh, Harvey, that's swell!" Lukie cried. "Is there anything the committee can do to help?"

"Yes," Harvey grinned. He was a lean boy, not much taller than Lukie, with long, thin hands and eyes that looked quizzical behind his thick glasses. "Promise not to razz us if we hit a few sour notes."

They both laughed.

"When will you know for sure, Harvey?" Lukie asked.

"Well — we've been rehearsing every night . . ."

He was interrupted by the bell.

"Look," he said, starting up the hall, "I've been sort of busy lately. Why don't you stop by the news agency some night and we'll talk?"

The remainder of the day flew by in a series of warm triumphs for Lukie. In her sixth-hour Latin class, Mr. Panella, who was also the Student Council adviser, complimented her on her homecoming presentation, and when the last bell rang, everybody crowded around her with an encouraging word. It was as if an exciting new dimension had been added to her life, and she wondered to herself if she was finally developing a personality.

"Pay more attention to your smile, Lukie," Sally coached her as the two of them collected their books and started for home. "You smile with your eyes. You should smile with your mouth — you know, real wide, like Lorena Pearsall."

It was a bright October afternoon. The whistle was blowing at the Western Knitting Mill. Bells clanged from

15

the depot, where the North Star, the sleek, royal blue streamliner that ran from Detroit all the way up to the Straits of Mackinac, was gliding to a stop. The girls cut across the terraced high school lawn, talking excitedly about tests and teachers and who was taking whom to the homecoming dance. Junior Rosenquist had asked her, Sally said, but she'd turned him down — sort of. Not that Junior was a drip or anything, she explained, but he was always showing off, and sometimes it embarrassed her to be his date.

"When are you going over to Harvey's, Lukie?" Sally asked.

"I don't know." Lukie shrugged. "Some night next week. Why don't you come with me?"

"Oh, *hon*estly, Lukie!" Sally exclaimed, exasperated. "You've got to stop being so *shy* about boys!"

At the corner of Fourth and Wilcox, they waved good-bye and went their separate ways. Lukie turned up Wilcox Street, past Bebout's IGA to the cemetery. Going by Bebout's, she struck a pose and looked at her reflection in the window. Not enough chin, she thought, studying her face, and the eyes were too large. She moved closer to the window and practiced smiling — first with her lips closed, then with her teeth showing — tenderly, seductively, demurely. It was no use, she decided; she was stuck with what she had — and then she noticed Mr. Bebout grinning at her from inside the store. She blushed and hurried on her way.

She thought of her encounter with Harvey Toles and felt a tingle of excitement run through her. She'd never had a boyfriend, or even a real date, for that matter, where the boy brought you a corsage and promised your father not to keep you out late. But she barely knew Harvey, really. He and his father had moved to Zebron Falls the year before Lukie started high school. His mother was dead, and there was talk that his father had been in a sanatorium with tuberculosis, and that running the news agency was all the work he could do. Even so, she felt a certain fondness for Harvey, a kind of — affinity. Three summers ago he had been painfully injured at the village park, and she had been to blame — although no one knew it except Billy. It had been an accident, but still it had been her fault, and the scars on Harvey's forehead always made her feel guilty.

The fallen leaves in the cemetery were ankle-deep, and there was a pleasant autumn haze in the air. In the distance, the sun glittered off the silos at Great Oaks. If Harvey's band played at the dance, she thought, there'd be little chance of his asking her to be his date. But — it didn't matter. Dates weren't that important. It was just as much fun dancing with the boys in the stag line, and there weren't any complications about parking up on Squirrel Road afterward.

Still — with Harvey Toles, maybe she wouldn't mind the complications.

4

The Tuesday Musicale, which was directed by Miss Eula Pray, the town librarian, rehearsed above Crissman's Drugs, in the old Zebron Falls Opera House. Lukie enjoyed the rehearsals. Miss Pray, a tiny, vibrant woman, always had something new for them to try out, an English madrigal, perhaps, or a flamenco piece; and afterward they would all stroll over to the Sweet Shoppe for Cokes and French fries — Lukie and Sally, Billy and Junior, who constituted the Musicale's youth chorus. Sometimes Miss Pray would join them and talk of the time she'd played in *The Girl of the Golden West* with a touring company, or of the year she'd lived as a Bohemian in Chicago. Miss Pray was a great favorite with the young people of the town.

One night, when Lukie was studying at the library, Miss Pray came up to her in a dither. A minor crisis had occurred in the Musicale, she said. Beatrice LaBurge, the group's piano accompanist, had developed a touch of arthritis in her fingers. Rehearsals would have to be canceled until a replacement could be found.

"Everybody says your friend Harvey Toles is a brilliant musician. Do you think he'd be interested?"

"Golly, Miss Pray, I don't know. He's not really my friend."

"But he's playing for the homecoming dance, isn't he?"

"I hope so," Lukie replied uncertainly, "but I'm not sure."

Miss Pray patted Lukie's hand.

"Why don't you stop by the news agency tonight and talk to him?" she suggested. "You have a nice way about you, dear. I'm sure he'll accept."

Lukie's heart gave a leap. Harvey Toles in the Tuesday Musicale! — and it would be a relief to get rid of Mrs. LaBurge, who wrote the "Town Tattler" column in the *Clarion* and was always prying into their affairs. She looked at the clock. Eight-thirty, and her week-night curfew was nine. There was still time. She plunked her books down on Miss Pray's desk.

"Would you keep my books for me, Miss Pray? I'll pick them up in the morning."

Lukie not only saw Harvey Toles that night, she collided with him — as he came around the corner of Third and Main, wheeling a wooden pushcart. Lukie went sprawling.

"Lukie!" Harvey cried, helping her to her feet. "Are you hurt?"

"Golly, Harvey," Lukie said, rubbing her knees, "you sure bowl a girl over."

19

"Gee, I'm sorry," Harvey apologized. "I don't see too well at night."

"It's all right," Lukie said, flustered. "I was just coming to see you, anyway."

"About the dance?" Harvey asked. "It's all set. We might have to play some of the arrangements twice, but there'll be enough to fill the dance cards."

"Oh, swell, Harvey!" Lukie smiled. "Can you do 'Jersey Bounce'?"

"Yes, and 'In the Mood.' We've even got a dance version of Mr. Leiber's victory song."

"Do you play the violin with the band?"

"No, just the piano. I never play the violin at school. The kids think it's — you know, square." Harvey returned to the pushcart. "Come on. I've got to pick up the out-of-state papers at the depot."

As they walked up Main Street, Lukie told him about the situation in the Tuesday Musicale.

"Sure, I'll do it," Harvey agreed. "I've wanted to play in the Musicale ever since we moved to Zebron Falls, but I figured you were all sort of — well, snooty."

"Why on earth did you think that!" Lukie said in amazement.

"I don't know." Harvey shrugged. "Your crowd sort of runs things at school — you and Sally, Billy and Junior."

Lukie started giggling.

"What's so funny?" Harvey asked.

"Nothing — it's just that all along I've thought *you* were snooty."

"Me?" Harvey's face had a wry look. "Boy, that's a laugh!"

"Well, you never go to any of the parties, and you always seem kind of — aloof."

"It's just that I'm always so busy. My dad isn't too strong, and I help out a lot at the agency. And then twice a week I study privately."

"With Mr. Leiber?" Lukie asked.

"Yes. He's a very brilliant man. He used to play with the Detroit Symphony."

He rambled on about his music, casually mentioning great composers and using complicated musical terms. He was working on the Tchaikovsky concerto, he said, with Mr. Leiber doing the orchestral parts on the piano. For a minute, Lukie thought Harvey Toles might be conceited and then decided it was just his enthusiasm.

"You really like music," she said, "don't you?"

"Yes," Harvey replied, rather shyly. "It sort of — does things to me. It's hard to explain."

"I know," Lukie said. "I feel that way about dirt."

"Dirt?"

"You know, earth — in my vegetable garden. When I stick my hands in the soil and let it run through my fingers, nothing else seems important."

"Do you tend the garden all by yourself?" Harvey asked.

"Of course. I do all sorts of things. I even lay bricks."

"Maybe I could walk you home from school some day," Harvey suggested, timidly, "and you could show me your garden."

"All right," Lukie agreed. "And maybe you'd like to come to my open-house after the homecoming game. You can sample one of my homemade cakes."

"Hey!" Harvey grinned. "That'd be swell!"

They stopped to look at the new display of winter fashions in Mitzelfeld's window. Across the street, voices echoed from the hotel, where the monthly meeting of the Businessmen's Association was letting out. Lukie spotted her father and felt a sinking sensation go through her. It was past her curfew. She tried to duck in Mitzelfeld's doorway, but it was too late.

"Young lady!" her father called across the street. "Do you realize what time it is?"

Lukie felt mortified.

"It's my father," she explained to Harvey. "I'm supposed to be in by nine on school nights. Well — so long, Harvey. I guess I'll probably be seeing you at Tuesday Musicale."

"You'll be seeing me before that."

"I will?" Lukie said, confused.

"At school tomorrow, silly."

They both laughed.

"Come along home, young lady!" Her father's voice was louder this time. "This instant!"

"Well — good night, Harvey."

"Good night, Lukie," Harvey said, and then called after her, "Hey, how come everybody calls you 'Lukie'?"

"It's really 'Lucinda,' " Lukie called back. "I used to be called 'Lucy,' but when my little brother pronounced it, it came out 'Lukie' — and it stuck."

And then she hurried across the street, her head bent down to conceal her tears. Her cheeks burned with embarrassment. He had humiliated her in front of Harvey Toles, she thought hotly — and in that moment she wished her father dead.

5

Billy Butts was a senior at Zebron High, a year ahead of Lukie. He was captain of the football team and president of the Student Council. Everybody was fond of Billy Butts, and when he strolled up Main Street in that jaunty way of his, it was a kind of event. "Hey, Billy!" people would call from Crissman's Drugs and Mitzelfeld's Department Store, and Billy would grin and wave and stop to exchange a few words about Saturday's game. Just his passing by seemed to make people feel better, for Billy had promised it would be a championship season, and the town loved him, as it had loved the Buttermilk Twins — as it loved all of its heroes.

Billy and his parents lived at the end of Old Perch Road, in the rambling fieldstone superintendent's house at Great Oaks Farm. Great Oaks was one of the finest livestock and dairy farms in the state — three hundred acres of rolling pastures and wooded ravines, stocked with magnificent herds of Guernseys and Aberdeen Angus. A spring-fed creek wound through the pastures and emptied into the river. White-tailed deer browsed in the ravines, and a flock of mallards wintered in the creek, which never stopped running.

The Butts family had been a fixture at Great Oaks for so long the town had almost — but not quite — forgotten they were colored — the only Negro family in Zebron Falls. Lukie had never known any Negroes other than the Buttses. She had seen many others, in the movies, mostly, but the movie Negroes all looked alike and talked alike and had shiny round faces. Billy and his parents were different. Ella Butts was slender and light-skinned, with soft angular features — like a Creole, Uncle Farnie had once observed. Billy and his father, Henry Butts, were much darker, with a dusty gray tint to their skin, like a pastel.

Lukie and Billy had grown up together, had skated the river together, had even been quarantined for scarlet fever together — at Lukie's house, for Billy had been there the day she came down with the symptoms. She still remembered the crimson rash on her face and the hot pain in her throat and the formaldehyde smell of the candles the men from the Health Department had burned in the house to kill the germs. She'd felt sure she was going to die, but once the disease had run its course, she'd found that being quarantined had its advantages. Having Billy in the house was like having a big brother, even though they were both too sick to have much fun.

At times it seemed Billy had a million friends, but

Lukie knew his breezy manner was simply his way of keeping people at arm's length without their knowing it. Except for Junior Rosenquist. Junior, who was Lukie's age, idolized Billy. Last summer, the two of them had spent long hours in the south pasture, practicing drop-kicks and reverses; and in the varsity games Billy would frequently carry the ball down to the goal line, then let Junior take it in for the touchdown — for he knew that Junior's father, who owned the Studebaker dealership opposite the depot, wanted his son to attend the university at Ann Arbor and be an All-American. It was as if Billy was embarrassed over being a better player than Junior, and whenever Junior told tall stories at the Sweet Shoppe, Billy never contradicted him.

"He's got enough problems," Billy said, "trying to live up to his old man's expectations that he be the big cheese of Zebron High."

But as the homecoming game grew near, and it became evident that Zebron High was heading for a showdown with Pontiac, the perennial West Conference champions, there was speculation that Junior's star was about to fade — that in the big game he could expect no favors from his friend Billy Butts.

"Billy's going to be so busy with those big brutes from Pontiac," said Addison Carey, the team manager, "Junior will be lucky to get past the line of scrimmage."

The gossip upset Lukie, so that evening she walked over to Great Oaks. Billy, still in his varsity jacket, was coming out of the heifer barn. He spotted Lukie coming up the pasture and jogged down to meet her.

"Rag Apple Bess is going to calve tonight," he called to

her. "Tomorrow, at the latest."

"Again!" Lukie exclaimed. Rag Apple Bess was the farm's prize-winning Guernsey. "Golly, it seems just yesterday she was being born herself."

"Yeah." Billy nodded. "And you were so scared you hid in the straw."

"I was not scared!" Lukie protested. "I just thought she was going to be born dead, that's all."

Billy grinned. "My old man sure had his hands full that night," he said, "with ol' Rag Apple coming out feet first and you bawling in the straw." He took Lukie's hand. "Come on, ol' buddy, let's take a walk."

They started down toward the river.

"I wish we'd never sold off our farm," Lukie said wistfully. "I'd like to raise some Guernseys."

"Heck, that's easy enough," Billy said. "Start a farm of your own."

"Oh, Billy." Lukie scoffed. "Girls don't start farms."

"You could," Billy said. "You've got the touch."

Dusk was creeping over the valley. The sound of cowbells drifted out from the barns. It was a quiet autumn evening, cool and clear, with a mist rising from the river. Billy seemed restless.

"Getting nervous over the homecoming game?" Lukie asked.

"A little," Billy said with a shrug. "But it's nothing. It goes away."

"Are you in pretty good shape? I mean, last Saturday I thought sure you'd broken your back, the way they all piled on top of you."

Billy went into a little act. "Good shape?" he said,

pained. He held a hand up to his forehead as if he'd been insulted. "Why, I'm a regular Tom Harmon, I'm in such good shape!"

And then he broke into an imaginary touchdown run, racing up a little rise in the pasture, a twisting, weaving silhouette against the darkening sky. Lukie, giggling with delight, fell in with Billy's mood. "Well, I'm Red Grange," she called after him, "and your number's up, Tom!" She chased after him and, at the top of the rise, leaped up on his back and began tickling him. The two of them collapsed in laughter and tumbled down the pasture, arms akimbo and Lukie's skirt flying. They laughed till their sides hurt, then lay in the sharp-smelling rye grass, catching their breath.

"Oh, Billy." Lukie sighed. "I never want to graduate. I want to stay in high school forever."

"Naw." Billy scowled. "High school's hard."

"Yes, hard," Lukie agreed, "but nice."

"By the way," Billy said, "I got my application from Ann Arbor in the mail today."

Lukie rolled over on her side and looked seriously at him.

"Have you decided what you're going to major in?"

"Engineering, probably — if I don't get drafted."

"But you'll get an academic deferment, won't you?"

"For a year or two." Billy got to his feet and extended a hand to Lukie. "But — who knows?"

When they reached the river, they automatically turned up a path that led to one of their old fishing spots — a dead elm that had fallen into the water. Billy took off his jacket and spread it out for Lukie to sit on.

"You'll be cold," she objected.

"That's okay. It'll toughen me up for Pontiac."

"Billy," Lukie said, "there's been a lot of talk about Junior — that he won't be able to pull his weight and the game is going to be a one-man show."

"Don't worry about Junior. He'll do just fine."

"Are we going to win, Billy? I mean, Pontiac has such a strong team."

Billy grinned and took out the rabbit's foot that he always carried with him.

"Give it a little rub, Lukie," he said. "It's going to need all the rubbing it can get."

"I'm serious, Billy," Lukie persisted. "Do we really have a chance?"

Billy looked at Lukie for a moment.

"We're going to win it in the first series of plays," he said firmly. "But the toss of the coin has got to go our way."

"I don't understand." Lukie frowned.

"I've got a little scheme." Billy smiled mysteriously. "Now rub the rabbit's foot, Lukie. Rub it hard."

6

Since it was Friday night — fish-fry night — the tap room was filled to capacity. Mr. Cromie, the bartender, was run off his feet, mixing highballs and drawing pitchers of beer that foamed down the sides. There was much gaiety and laughter, and the tune playing on the jukebox was lost in the noise.

Heil! heil! right in der Führer's face!

Lukie stood on her toes to see over the crowd. Uncle Farnie's cronies from the volunteer fire company waved to her from the bar and pointed to a booth up near the window. As Lukie had expected, Uncle Farnie was entertaining one of the new girls from the knitting mill. Uncle Farnie was forever pursuing aimless flirtations with the mill girls, none of which had ever progressed beyond the tap room.

"Oh, yes." The girl smiled politely when Uncle Farnie

introduced her to Lukie. "You're the one with the dog and the vegetable garden."

And then, with a nudge from Uncle Farnie, the girl excused herself and left the two of them alone.

"She's cute," Lukie commented approvingly. "Is it anything serious?"

Uncle Farnie was a carbon copy of Lukie's father, only slightly smaller and boyish, rather than stern. He had wavy brown hair, and melancholy blue eyes that lit up when he smiled.

"You know how it is, sweetheart," he said noncommittally. "Ships that pass in the night."

"Oh, honestly, Uncle Farnie." Lukie shook her head. "Sometimes I just don't understand you. I mean, haven't you ever had a — a great r*omance,* or anything?"

"Oh, I've had my moments." Her uncle winked.

"Really?" Lukie said eagerly. "Anyone I know?"

"Maybe. She's still in town. One winter we skated twenty bridges up the river. It's the record." He smiled over the memory. "She had a hole in one of her mittens, which gave me an excuse for holding her hand."

"Why, how lovely!" Lukie smiled. "Whatever happened to her?"

"Oh, she got married while I was out bumming around the country."

Uncle Farnie signaled to one of the waitresses.

"A sarsaparilla for my best girl!" he called, and then returned to Lukie. "But you didn't come down here to check up on my love life."

"We-ell," Lukie began, "as a matter of fact —"

She told him about her plans for the Buttermilk Twins.

31

Uncle Farnie listened intently, then said:

"You mean you want me up on a float with your daddy?"

"Well, yeah, that was the general idea."

"With the whole town watching?"

"Uh-huh."

Uncle Farnie stared vacantly at his drink. For a second, Lukie worried that he'd already had too much and wouldn't remember anything in the morning.

"Does this mean a lot to you, sweetheart?" he asked finally.

"Yes, Uncle Farnie, it means an awful lot."

He sighed wearily.

"All right," he agreed. "But only if it's okay with your daddy, too."

"Oh, thank you, Uncle Farnie!" Lukie beamed. She leaned over and kissed her uncle on the cheek. "Everything will work out fine. You'll see."

But at supper the next day, Lukie's scheme crumbled in ruins. It was the first time her father had been home on time all week, and, nervously, she seized on the opportunity to present her plan. The words tumbled out. She had the familiar feeling that he wasn't listening, that what she had to say was stupid and unimportant, and it all came out in a rush. When she had finished, Walter Bishop set down his knife and fork and looked at her.

"Now listen to me carefully, Lukie," he said. "I'm going to be in Washington that weekend. We're bidding on a new Navy contract — caps, mittens, jerseys, enough to keep the mill going for a year or more. So it's out of the question."

"Couldn't somebody else do the bidding?" Lukie asked.

"No," her father answered firmly. "It's the manager's responsibility."

"But couldn't you do it some other time?"

"The United States Navy," Walter Bishop said impatiently, "is not about to adjust its schedule to accommodate the Zebron High football team. There's a war on, in case you haven't heard."

"Yes, sir," Lukie said. Then, in an effort to salvage at least a partial victory, she added, "But if you didn't have to go to Washington — would you do it then?"

"But I *am* going to Washington," her father replied, "and so the question is irrelevant."

He took a sip of water and looked sternly at Lukie.

"Now let me ask *you* a question, young lady. Would you kindly explain why you haven't finished the storm windows yet?"

"But I did finish them," Lukie protested.

"Then you'd better do them again," her father ordered. "Half of them look as if they've been splattered with mud."

Lukie's eyes filled with tears. She threw down her napkin and got to her feet, her lips quivering.

"Well, if they do," she said between her sobs, "it's because a certain somebody went to work the day of the storm and left the garage door open!" And then she fled from the room.

"Young lady!" her father called after her. "Come back here this instant!"

But Lukie kept going, up the back stairway to her room. She slammed the door behind her and threw her-

33

self on the bed. In a few minutes, her mother brought up a plate.

"Finish your dinner, dear," she said gently. "I made these croquettes especially for you."

Lukie blew her nose and wiped her eyes.

"Oh, Mama, why does he keep picking on me like that! I get good grades and do my chores and look after Beth and Buddy. What more does he expect of me?"

"He's been under a lot of pressure at the mill, dear. The union is trying to get in. Give him time."

"Time? But I'm nearly seventeen years old, Mama. How much time does he need?"

"Fathers are strange creatures, dear. Sometimes they have difficulty in coming to terms with their children."

"But he treats Beth like his little darling and lets Buddy get away with murder."

"I know." Myrene Bishop stroked her daughter's hair. "I'll talk to him, dear. He'll come round. Just be patient."

Later that night, Lukie slipped out of the house and went to her place above the river, still brooding. She would show him, she thought as she walked down through the orchard. After she graduated, she would go away to a big city and get a glamorous job — as a fashion designer, perhaps, or on a magazine. Then one day she would return in triumph, in heels and a tailored suit, and stay at the St. James Hotel, and he would regret all the mean things he'd done to her.

Her thoughts went back to the incident of her portrait. Her mother, who had studied art in college, had painted it, in oils, with Lukie posed in her communion dress on the little wicker stool in the sunroom. It had hung in the parlor, above the mantel, and then one day her father took it down. Beth and Buddy were growing up, he said, and the prominence of their big sister's portrait might make them resentful. But Lukie had suspected a different motive — that deep down he didn't really love her.

She came out of the orchard and started up the river to her hidden path. The sky was clear and the stars were out. The best sky in the world, Uncle Farnie had once called it. She breathed in the cool night air and felt her resentment draining away. It was hard to stay mad out-of-doors. No, she would never go away. She would spend the rest of her life in Zebron Falls, as would Billy and Sally and Junior — yes, and Harvey, for he was a part of their crowd now, too. They would raise families and grow into positions of responsibility, running the clubs and the schools and the Village Board, helping to make the town better than it was before. That was how it had always been with the young people of Zebron Falls, all the way back to Joshua Zebron and the early settlers, and that was how it would be with them. It was the one great certainty of her life.

Maybe she tried too hard, she thought; maybe that was it. Well, if her father was interested in coming to terms, she was available. But she was tired of going to him.

7

In late October, Indian summer came to Zebron Falls. It was a wonderful time of year. Lukie and Sally fell into a routine of staying late at school, to work on the floats and decorate the gym for the dance, and then walking home in the autumn dusk, with lights glowing from the houses and the smell of burning leaves in the air.

Sometimes they would stroll over to Halbach Field and watch Billy and Junior practicing the special plays Coach Ennis was saving for the Pontiac game. The plays were very complicated, and as the days grew shorter the scrimmages lasted till it was too dark to see the ball — and then the clatter of cleats would echo through the darkening streets as the exhausted players jogged back to the school for steaming showers and liniment rubs in the gymnasium locker room. They would sing fight songs in the shower and swat each other's rumps with wet towels.

Throughout the season, Billy Butts had dazzled the

crowds with the audacity of his broken-field running —
teasing would-be tacklers, taunting them, like a cat playing with a mouse, and then, in a flash of speed, slipping
away and racing, untouched, into the end zone. He had
brought Zebron High through seven straight games, un-
defeated and unscored against. Now only Pontiac separated the school from its first championship since the
golden era of the Buttermilk Twins, and the town was at
a fever pitch.

Two days before the game, Lukie and Sally stopped by
the Sweet Shoppe for cherry Cokes. Lukie had never
seen the place so jammed. A huge BEAT PONTIAC!
streamer filled the mirror behind the soda fountain, and
a new Glenn Miller record blared from the jukebox —
about a gal in Kalamazoo who was a real pipperoo. It
was a fine song that made you want to dance, and the fact
that it was about Michigan made everybody feel special.

Billy and Junior came by after practice that day, in
their varsity jackets and with their hair still wet from their
showers. Junior sat next to Sally, who proceeded to ig-
nore him. Billy sat next to Lukie — Billy always sat next
to Lukie — and the two of them went over the homecoming schedule.

Everything was ready for the bonfire, Lukie reported,
and Holland's Florists was donating roses for the queen
and her court. But Harvey was having a problem with
the music stands, he needed some luminous paint for the
lettering.

"Case's Hardware," Billy said. "It comes in a little can.
Mr. Case will probably give it to him for free. Now, what
about your dad?"

Lukie shook her head. "It's no use, Billy. He'll be out of town the whole weekend, and Uncle Farnie won't do it without him."

"Well," Billy said, "it was a good idea."

He seemed quiet and withdrawn, Lukie thought, as if something was bothering him.

"Are you going to the dance, Billy?" she asked.

"I don't know. Rag Apple's calf has got some kind of infection. My dad and I are taking turns in the barn. What about you? Has Harvey asked you for a date?"

"No." Lukie blushed.

Billy gave her an exasperated look. "Well, I don't blame him," he said irritably, "the way you're always running around in those dirty jeans and with your face all muddied up from your garden. Sometimes you're a regular hayseed, you know that?"

Lukie looked up at Billy, astonished. He had never spoken to her this way before.

"You're not a kid anymore, ol' buddy. I mean, you're starting to get a pretty good shape on you, and . . ."

Lukie waited for him to go on, but he just stirred his Coke and said nothing.

"And what, Billy?" she asked softly.

"Never mind," Billy answered, avoiding Lukie's eyes.

"Billy, what's got into you, anyway? Is it the game?"

Billy slouched down in the booth. "I guess so. Everything's falling apart."

"But you've been telling the whole town we're going to win."

"What do you expect me to tell them? That we're going to lose our shirts? I mean, when you're the captain, the load is all on your shoulders, and sometimes it gets pretty heavy."

The team was taut and edgy, he told her. Tempers had flared, and there had been clumsy mistakes in scrimmage. Junior had come down with a bad case of butterfingers, and Coach Ennis was worried that the game would be lost before it began.

"It's just nerves, Billy," Lukie said reassuringly. "They'll snap out of it. You said so yourself. And the parade will boost everybody's morale."

"Yeah." Billy gave a weak grin. "There's nothing like a parade."

The parade was a great success, coming up Main Street in double time, with the band playing, and the drums beating, and the pompom girls, in their tight satin outfits, kicking their legs high — and, above, the sky orange from the glow of the bonfire. Billy rode in the back of Mr. B. F. Higbie's Packard convertible, in his football uniform, waving his helmet to the crowd.

"Go, Billy, go!" the crowd yelled.

The parade units moved smartly up South Hill and into Eberline's pasture for the climactic rally. Lukie was waiting at the pasture gate to make sure the floats were parked a safe distance from the bonfire. Sally, who had ridden on the junior class float, ran up to her excitedly.

"Guess what!" she said, out of breath. "I'm going to let Junior take me to the dance after all."

Lukie broke into a giggle.

"But I thought you said Junior was a pill," she teased.

"Oh, *hon*estly, Lukie, it's only because he's worked so hard getting ready for the game. I mean, what was I supposed to do? Besides," Sally added with a blush, "he wrote me a nice poem."

The rally unfolded with much enthusiasm, but Lukie sensed that something was lacking, something she couldn't quite pinpoint. The band played the Alma Mater, and then Addison Carey, with a megaphone, led the crowd in a rousing cheer for Billy.

"Give me a *B!* Give me an *I!* Give me an *L-L-Y!*"

The crowd urged Mr. Leiber, a rotund little man who resembled a German burgomaster, to play his new victory song, but he declined.

"We want the song to become a tradition for the school," he explained. "And so it will be played only when the team is assured of victory. Otherwise it would have no meaning."

There were speeches by Coach Ennis and Mr. Panella, and then a hush came over the crowd as Mr. Severence, the principal, stepped forward.

"Perhaps the great value of sports," he began, "is that they teach us how to lose, for life is filled with disappointments. But the important thing is the integrity of the effort, to do our best and have no regrets . . ."

He spoke through the megaphone, and as his words echoed out over the pasture, it dawned on Lukie what was wrong with the rally. They were going to lose. It came over her with a dreadful certainty. Despite all the rah-rah and Billy's rabbit's foot, they were going to lose, and Mr. Severence was preparing them for it.

". . . and so regardless of the outcome tomorrow, you will be heroes, for you will have done your best, and your best is all that we can ask of you, or that you can ask of yourselves."

There were a few final cheers, and then the rally started breaking up. Horns tooted and engines revved noisily. Lukie bit her lip and hurried across the crowded pasture. It wasn't fair, she thought, and that night she huddled in the dormer windowseat, grieving — for Billy, for Junior, for all the might-have-beens.

8

Under a blue Michigan sky — the best sky in the world — the Zebron High football squad, fighting a bad case of the jitters, took to the field.

The band played, the crowd roared, and the cheerleaders cartwheeled in the autumn sun.

"Ladies and gentlemen, here are the starting lineups . . . "

Billy ran the team downfield in a quick warmup. Junior kept glancing over at the visitors' side of the field. The Pontiac players, in their bright red jerseys, looked like giants.

"For Zebron Falls — at fullback, George L. Rosenquist, Jr. — at quarterback, William G. Butts . . ."

The team went through a mock scrimmage, then trotted over to the sideline for a final conference with Coach Ennis. Once the game began, they knew, they would be on their own; the coach never sent in plays from the bench.

"They'll be ganging up on you, Billy. Play it tight. Junior — no fumbling. When these boys hit, they hit hard."

The pregame ceremonies were commencing. The band played the national anthem. Amid great pomp, Lorena Pearsall, the homecoming queen, was escorted to a seat of honor. There was a moment of silent prayer for the boys overseas, and then the referee signaled for the crucial tossing of the coin. Billy, as team captain, buckled his helmet and started out to midfield — then suddenly changed his mind and grabbed Junior.

"You do it, sport," he said. "I don't want to press my luck."

"But, Billy . . ." Junior gasped.

"Go *on*, Junior!" Billy said, shoving him out onto the field.

"But how should I call it — heads or tails?"

"Whichever comes into your mind," Billy ordered. "Now get going!"

Billy shut his eyes, waiting for the loudspeakers to boom the outcome of his gamble.

"Ladies and gentlemen — Zebron High will defend the south goal and has elected to receive."

Billy let out a whoop. Then, with much yelling and shaking of fists, the team ran down to the south goal and went into a huddle. One of the boys began crying and couldn't stop.

43

"Oh, Billy, what if we lose!"

And then Billy uncorked his scheme.

"Okay, guys, after we get the ball, no huddles, understand? Line up as fast as you can. We'll run Thirteen-A on every down . . ."

"On every down?" Junior asked, wide-eyed. "Are you sure about that, Billy?"

"Yeah, Junior, I'm sure. We've got to do the unexpected. Okay, hup, two, three — let's go!"

The two teams lined up in a blur of color — the maize and blue of Zebron High and the red and white of Pontiac. The gun went off, and with drums rolling and pennants waving, the ball sailed down the field, straight and true.

The championship game had begun.

Billy took the ball on the five-yard line. A platoon of blockers immediately formed in front of him. "Let's roll, Billy!" Junior hollered. "Let's roll!" The jitters were gone now, and the team moved upfield like a phalanx, blocking low to offset their weight disadvantage — to the twenty, the thirty, before Billy came crashing down on the thirty-seven.

"We're hot!" Billy yelled. "We're hot!"

Quickly, the team scrambled into position, allowing Pontiac scant time to set its defense, and before the crowd realized what was happening, the visitors had been put to rout. Thirteen-A was one of the razzle-dazzle plays that Billy and Junior had practiced all summer in the south pasture — a double reverse followed by a Statue of Liberty, with either Billy or Junior faking the pass. The first call went to Junior, who knifed over left guard down into

44

Pontiac territory, dragging two tackles with him. Then it was Billy's turn. The handoff went from Billy to the left halfback and then to Junior, who faded back as if to pass. The Pontiac line fell for the strategy a second time and came charging in on him. Then, just as Junior was about to be smothered, Billy materialized from out of nowhere, snatched the ball from Junior's outstretched arm, and rolled around right end — twisting and weaving through the secondary, then streaking downfield. The last defender between him and the end zone made a desperate dive and caught Billy by the ankles, but it was too late. He came down with the ball two feet across the goal line.

A great roar went up from the stands — but it would be the last cheer to echo from Halbach Field for the remainder of the first half. Billy's drop-kick for the extra point was blocked. The ball took a bad bounce and careened wildly upfield. There was a mad scramble. Pontiac recovered on the Zebron High forty-nine. Within minutes, the game was turned around. Pontiac marched inexorably down the field, like a parent scolding an errant child. The visitors scored on a line plunge, and the kick for the extra point was good.

ZEBRON FALLS 6   VISITORS 7

The game settled into a bruising defensive standoff. Neither team was able to penetrate the other's territory. Billy and Junior were everywhere, plugging holes, anticipating plays, batting down passes. Then, in the closing minutes of the half, Pontiac mounted another drive, down to the eighteen. The Zebron High line stiffened and held, but the intruders were still within field-goal range. Billy and Junior put a desperate rush on the kicker, but the ball sailed squarely through the uprights. And as the half ended, the maize and blue of Zebron High knew they had finally met their match.

ZEBRON FALLS 6   VISITORS 10

"Oh, Billy. I don't know if I can hold up." Junior sighed wearily as they trudged up to the locker room.

"You can do it, Junior. Just think of the dance tonight — the soft lights, the sweet music, Sally in your arms."

"Fat chance," Junior said gloomily. "After Pontiac gets through mopping up the field with us, she probably won't even speak to me."

"Junior," Billy said impatiently, "you must've been out to lunch when they passed out brains. I told you from the start we're going to win, didn't I?"

"Yeah, but have you decided exactly how we're going to do it?"

"Don't worry." Billy threw an arm around Junior. "We'll figure something out."

But the second half proved as frustrating as the first — a grueling, monotonous standoff that was beginning to take its toll of both teams. Finally, late in the fourth quarter, it appeared to be all over but the mourning. The Zebron High line, outweighed fifteen pounds per man, started to give. With the clock running out, it was Pontiac's ball on the Zebron High eight-yard line, first down and goal to go. A loud, rhythmic chant rose from the stands:

"Hold that line! Hold that line!"

Billy scampered up and down the line of scrimmage, clapping his hands, urging his exhausted players into an extra effort. The Pontiac fullback went straight up the middle for the kill. Three times. First to the five, then to the three, then to the one. The spectators were on their feet now. Fourth down and a yard. Could the team hold? It was all riding on this one play — the work, the sweat, the long hours of practice in the south pasture.

The fullback hit the line like a battering ram. There was the smacking sound of leather colliding with leather. And then a deafening roar split the air. The ball was on the one-foot line. Zebron High had held.

The band struck up Mr. Leiber's new victory song. The cheerleaders, laughing and crying at the same time, led the singing. And the entire stadium sensed that Zebron High's moment had finally come.

"Lift their banner proudly,
Sing their praises proudly,
The maize and the blue and the best!

"Let our hearts acclaim them,
As victory proclaims them,
The Champions of the West!"

The team formed a huddle in the end zone. Billy looked up at the clock. Four minutes and fifty seconds remaining in the game.

"Okay, guys, we've got a long way to go and not much time to get there. Hup, two, three — let's go!"

And then it began — the great drive that would go down in the history of Zebron High, the team battered and bone-weary, and Billy urging on the players with

47

sweet-talk and a slap on the rump. He fired a bullet pass to Junior on the twenty to give them breathing room — and then it was Junior again, grinding it out up the middle, a few yards here, a few there, and oh, if they could only lie down and rest! Twice they came up with long yardage on third down, and twice they made it. Then on the Pontiac forty-five, Billy called an end run and got trapped behind the line of scrimmage. Desperate, he circled back to his own thirty, then the twenty, then zigzagged back and forth across the field, his jersey torn to shreds and the entire Pontiac line in hot pursuit. His shoulder pads flapped noisily, and his dusty black skin, shiny with sweat, glistened in the waning sun.

Junior had been knocked flat at the beginning of the play. Now, as he looked up and saw Billy's predicament, he leaped to his feet and raced back to rescue his friend.

"Let's roll, Billy!" he hollered, gliding in ahead of him and straight-arming two Pontiac linemen. "Let's roll!"

They battered their way back to the midfield stripe and then down into Pontiac territory, but the red jerseys were closing in fast and forcing them over to the sideline.

"Sixteen-B, Junior!" Billy shouted. "Sixteen-B!"

Immediately, Junior fell back a few paces behind Billy, who kept racing down the sideline, on a collision course with three Pontiac defenders. Two of the red jerseys lunged for him. Billy waited till the last possible moment, then flipped a lateral to Junior, who cut diagonally downfield and went into the end zone standing up.

The crowd screamed hysterically. Billy's kick for the extra point was good. The gun went off. It was all over. The crowd swarmed onto the field. The goal posts started coming down. The band struck up the victory song again. Coach Ennis was ecstatic. "Giant killers," he called Billy and Junior, thereby dubbing them for posterity. He was going to retire Billy's number, he said, and hang his shredded jersey in the trophy case in the Main Hall, next to the picture of the Buttermilk Twins.

And then the captain of the Pontiac team, a tall boy with freckles, pushed through the crowd and extended a hand to Billy.

"You deserved to win," he said. "You earned every yard of it."

Billy was so moved he didn't know what to say, and so he said nothing — just threw his arms around the Pontiac boy and slapped him on the back.

And then the Zebron High students swept Billy up on their shoulders, and Junior and Coach Ennis, and carried them off the field. All of Zebron Falls, it seemed, was exploding in celebration. Church bells rang, the siren atop the fire hall wailed, and the whistle at the Western Knitting Mill erupted in a series of shrill staccato salutes, spreading the word up and down the valley.

It had been a championship season.

9

And then cars loaded with celebrating students were skidding up the driveway at the house out on Old Perch Road, horns beeping and rear wheels spinning in the gravel. The house was filled with laughter and excitement. Everybody chattered all at once, about the game and the dance and the parties that would be held afterward — at Junior's and Miss Pray's and the Higbies'. Somebody cranked up the Victrola and put an Andrews Sisters record on to play.

> *Don't sit under the apple tree*
> *With anyone else but me,*
> *Till I come marching home!*

"Oh, isn't winning simply *won*derful!" cried Sally DeBaene.

The party had started in the sunroom, and then spilled into the dining room and the parlor — until even the front staircase was jammed with couples. Lukie's sister, Beth, hurried about, serving cider and popcorn and homemade doughnuts, while Buddy pestered all the football players for autographs. Lukie had baked an applesauce cake especially for Harvey Toles, but it vanished before he got so much as a crumb. Soon, even the cider started running low, and Myrene Bishop had to call Mr. Yates at the mill and ask him please to send around three more gallons right away.

"Good grief!" she exclaimed, hanging up the phone. "They'll eat us out of house and home!"

Lukie barely had a chance to have two words with Harvey. The crowd kept him occupied at the old upright piano in the sunroom. Finally, however, after Harvey had spilled cider down the front of his sweater, they had a moment alone in the kitchen.

"Boy, what a game!" Harvey said gleefully. "What a day!"

"Isn't it wonderful!" Lukie dabbed at the stains with a damp dish towel. "And it isn't even over yet."

"Look . . ." Harvey said awkwardly, "I was going to ask you to the dance, but since I'll be playing with the band and all — well, it wouldn't be fair for a guy to leave his date stranded."

"What makes you think I'd have gone with you?" Lukie said curtly.

An anxious look came into Harvey's eyes. Lukie had the feeling that it was all a new experience for him — the game, the party, his popularity with the crowd — and

51

that a rebuff would hurt his feelings terribly. Maybe he had never had a real date, either.

"Well, would you have?"

"Yes." She nodded, smiling. "I would have."

"Another time, maybe?"

"Yes, another time, Harvey." Lukie took his hand and led him out of the kitchen. "Come on, your fans are clamoring for more boogie-woogie."

Billy and Junior arrived at the head of a four-car caravan, horns blaring and tin cans trailing from the bumpers. There was a great commotion out on the front porch.

"*Bil*ly!" the girls squealed. "*Jun*ior!"

Billy looked very tired. His left wrist was taped up, and he walked with a limp. As he came up the lawn, Lukie noticed a melancholy look in his eyes, and suddenly she wanted the party to be over. Billy needed her, she sensed — and when Addison Carey suggested that everybody go down to the Sweet Shoppe, she felt relieved. Within seconds, the house was emptied. Car doors slammed. Somebody set off a firecracker. Lukie looked around for Harvey.

"He went back to town," Sally said, "to see if the paint is dry on the music stands."

Lukie felt disappointed that Harvey hadn't bothered to say goodbye.

"Come on, sport," Junior called to Billy as he piled into Addison Carey's '36 Ford. "Let's join the crowd."

"I think I'll skip it, Junior," Billy called back. "My bones still ache from that last tackle."

"Whatever you say," Junior agreed cheerfully. "See

52

you at the dance, huh? And don't forget my party!"

Billy and Lukie stood in the driveway and watched the cars roar out of sight. Junior stuck his head out the window of Addison Carey's Ford and waved. They waved back.

"Junior seems different," Lukie said. "He hardly showed off at all."

"He doesn't have to anymore," Billy replied. "Come on, ol' buddy, you can walk me home."

They started up the driveway and around the house.

"Poor Junior." Lukie sighed. "He'll be lost when you graduate."

"It'll only be for a year," Billy said.

They walked down toward the Lombardy poplars. The sun was setting in a blaze of lilac and gold. Thin layers of mist hung on the horizon. The leaves were almost gone from the trees, and there was a damp chill in the air. Soon the November rains would come, Lukie thought, and the countryside would be gray and bleak.

"Feeling blue, Billy?" she asked.

"A little, I guess."

"Is it the game?"

"Yeah." Billy nodded. "It's over, and I guess I don't want it to be."

Lukie knew that Billy wouldn't show up at Junior's party; that he probably wouldn't even stop by the dance. There were limits. The few times he'd gone to parties he had disappeared the minute the lights got turned off and the necking began. It was the same at the dances — a brief appearance, a grin and a wave, perhaps a little jitterbugging with Sally, but not regular dancing, where the boy held the girl in his arms. Nobody said anything about it; it was just the way things were, and you couldn't change them.

"Billy," Lukie said impulsively, "take me to the dance tonight. Please. We'll just sit in the balcony and watch."

"Is it really important to you?"

"Yes, Billy, it really is."

"Won't you have to be there early — you know, to get things organized?"

"Not really," Lukie said. "I have a well-trained committee."

"Okay." He smiled at her. "But let's go late and leave early."

Billy came by for Lukie at ten o'clock.

"Tell him I'll be right down, Mama!" Lukie called downstairs.

She fussed excitedly with the new taffeta dress her mother had made for her. It was almost like having a regular date, she thought. She wished she had a corsage. Instead, she tied a red ribbon in her hair.

"You'd better wear your warm coat, dear," her mother advised. "It's turning cold."

The night was crisp and clear, and there was a bright moon. The melancholy wail of a saxophone drifted out from the gym as Billy and Lukie crossed Wilcox Street to the school.

"Schools seem funny when they're empty, don't they?" Lukie said as they walked through the deserted corridors.

They slipped out onto the balcony without being seen. Billy pulled a wooden bench up to the railing for them to sit on. The gym was bathed in a soft light. The band was playing "Stardust." The musicians were surprisingly good, Lukie thought — two saxes, drums, a trumpet, a trombone, and Harvey, looking very purposeful at the piano. The music stands glittered like rhinestones.

HARVEY TOLES

and the

ARISTOCRATS

Lukie spotted Junior and Sally, dancing dreamily. It all seemed so lovely, she thought — and for a minute she felt left out.

"Phooey on everybody!" she whispered to Billy, taking his hand. "Let's go down and dance."

"No, Lukie."

"It'll be all right, Billy." Lukie tugged insistently at his arm. "Really it will."

There was a commotion down on the dance floor. While Billy and Lukie were arguing, the crowd had spotted them and lined up below the balcony. There was a rolling of drums and then a loud cheer.

"Give me a *B!* Give me an *I!* Give me an *L-L-Y!*"

Then the band broke into Mr. Leiber's victory song. They played it three times, and on the final chorus the crowd began pointing to the end of the balcony. Lukie looked around. Junior, in a tan sports jacket and dark brown pants, was loping toward them, with a grin a mile wide. He came to a stop in front of Billy. The two of them laughed self-consciously and horsed around for a minute. Then, arm-in-arm, they turned to face the crowd.

The gymnasium exploded in a roar that made the

crepe-paper decorations vibrate. Tears came to Lukie's eyes. She didn't know whether she was happy or sad, only that she was very, very proud of her friend Billy Butts.

The band was playing "Goodnight, Sweetheart" when Billy and Lukie started back to the house. Lukie fixed them hot cocoa and cinnamon toast. They sat in the sunroom, the lights turned low, and listened to a broadcast of dance music on the radio. And then the news came on. There were stories about a big naval battle in the Pacific, and about new government regulations for the rationing of tires, and about a bill in Congress that would lower the draft age to eighteen. It was midnight when Billy got up to leave.

"It's been a fine homecoming," Lukie said at the door, "hasn't it, Billy?"

"Yes, Lukie. It's been the best homecoming ever."

Lukie stood on her toes and kissed Billy lightly on the cheek.

"Don't ever leave Zebron Falls, Billy," she whispered. "I'd be lost without you to lean on."

Ever since they were children, Lukie and Billy had had a little ritual. On nights when they'd been out together they would flick their bedroom lights to signal they were home safe. The idea had come to Lukie when she was seven years old, the night she and Billy were allowed to go alone to the Hills Theater to see Jackie Cooper and Wallace Beery in *Treasure Island*. Walking home, everything had seemed spooky, and they had imagined pirates lurking in the shadows. Billy called it their "secret signal," and over the years it had become a routine with them.

And so, after Billy left, Lukie went up to her room, put on her nightgown, and watched at the window for his signal. But it never came. Several minutes passed. Then she saw something moving in the moonlight in the road. It was Billy on his bike, in overalls and with a large bucket dangling from the handlebars.

Lukie giggled with delight. He was going to do it himself, she thought. Everybody else had forgotten, so he was going to do it all by himself.

And in the morning, with church bells ringing, people paused in the streets to gaze up at the whitewashed proclamation that gleamed from the village water tower.

ZEBRON HIGH, '42

CHAMPIONS OF THE WEST!

That afternoon, a bank of dark gray clouds moved in from the north. A cold wind rattled the last of the leaves from the trees, and there were snow flurries.

Indian summer was over.

Part Two

10

Winter came early to Zebron Falls that year. The cold November rains turned quickly to snow. The snow fell thick and lovely, and by Thanksgiving the valley was blanketed in white.

On the seventh of December, a Monday, the town observed the first anniversary of the Japanese attack on Pearl Harbor. Memorial services were held at the high school, at which the new military Honor Roll was dedicated. It was a large bronze tablet, inscribed with a roster of all Zebron High graduates who had been called to the service of their country. Gold stars were affixed to the names of those who had been killed in action. The ceremony had an unsettling effect on Lukie. Ever since the conscription age had been lowered to eighteen, she had come to see the war as a growing threat to her personal world, and now she wondered how many of her friends' names would be inscribed in the tablet before the fighting was done — how many gold stars.

The war had brought many changes to Zebron Falls. Ration stamps were now required to purchase coffee, sugar, and gasoline; and there were reports that soon meat, canned goods, and shoes would be added to the list. One night at Tuesday Musicale, Mr. Panella came by the Opera House to invite the youth chorus to sing at the faculty Christmas party — and to announce his appointment as the official air-raid warden of Zebron Falls.

"But Mr. Panella," Sally puzzled afterward at the Sweet Shoppe, "how could an enemy possibly bomb the state of Michigan?"

"Oh, it would be quite simple," Mr. Panella replied matter-of-factly. He was a popular teacher, a dapper little man in his late forties and a confirmed bachelor. "By way of Iceland and Canada."

The Germans, he argued, sipping his chocolate soda, could easily equip a squadron of Stuka bombers with special fuel tanks. They could come in over Lake Superior, then drop down to treetop level, on a straight course for the great war plants of Detroit. He had written to the War Department about the possibility, he said, and suggested they install an antiaircraft battery up on South Hill, but nothing had come of it.

"My, what an interesting man," Miss Pray whispered to Lukie. "Does he sing?"

At first, the student body giggled at the sight of Mr. Panella climbing up to the high school bell tower, with his helmet and armband and binoculars, as well as a thick book on aircraft recognition that had been furnished by the Office of Civilian Defense. But after the papers were filled with stories of Japanese submarines shelling California and of Nazi saboteurs being set ashore on Long Island, he was taken more seriously. And it was at this point that Billy Butts decided to do a little matchmaking.

"Mr. Panella and Miss Pray!" Lukie gasped. "Billy, you can't be serious!"

"Think it over," Billy said with a grin. "They're both a little eccentric, and deep down Miss Pray is shy and lonely, even though she puts on a pretty good front."

Lukie marveled at how perceptive Billy was about people — and how tactful. A suggestion here, a suggestion there, and presto! Mr. Panella, who turned out to be a fine baritone, was invited to join the Musicale's adult choir. Soon he and Miss Pray were regularly observed at the St. James Hotel, in the tap room, or in the dining room for Sunday dinner. And on weekends, when Mr. Panella was on duty up in the bell tower, Miss Pray took him hot coffee and sandwiches. One Saturday, as Lukie and Billy were walking home from tobogganing, they heard Miss Pray's high-pitched laughter pealing out over Wilcox Street. Billy looked up at the bell tower and elbowed Lukie.

"I'll bet they're up there necking up a storm."

Perhaps because of the war, Lukie and her friends seemed to draw closer together, as if anticipating unavoidable changes in their lives. Sally frequently stayed overnight at Lukie's. Billy and Harvey, who would be graduating in June, made plans to room together in Ann Arbor. Junior proudly announced that he and Sally were going steady — and then amazed everyone still further by winning the school's creative writing competition, with a short story based on the homecoming game.

"Junior Rosenquist a writer!" Lukie said in amazement. "Who would have thought it!"

Harvey Toles proved an invaluable addition to the Tuesday Musicale, and it soon became evident that his was not an ordinary musical talent. Miss Pray referred·to him as "our budding genius" and regularly consulted him in matters of phrasing and harmony.

"One day that boy will own a Stradivarius," she predicted, "and perform in the great capitals of Europe."

The day before school let out for Christmas vacation, Harvey caught up to Lukie on the way home from school and asked if she would like to go to the show with him Saturday night. *Random Harvest* was playing, with Greer Garson and Ronald Coleman, and everybody said it was a swell picture.

"I'd love to, Harvey!" Lukie smiled brightly.

They had a fine time. The movie left Lukie with a warm glow, and as they walked home, Harvey held her hand. She considered inviting Harvey and his father to the house for Christmas dinner. They lived in an apartment above the news agency and probably would appreciate a big family holiday. But she decided against it, not wishing to risk being embarrassed again by her father. Instead, she invited Harvey to go along one day when she took Lady on her afternoon run.

"Wear your boots," she warned him. "The snow is pretty deep."

It was a gray, overcast day, and there was a cold wind. Lady flushed a pheasant out of the orchard — a ring-necked cock — then made a feeble attempt at a cottontail rabbit. It saddened Lukie to see her dog old and lame. In her youth, the huge German shepherd had raced the wind and swum the river, but now she gave chase with a frustrated whimper, as if wondering where it had all gone — the speed, the agility, the great stamina.

"How old is she?" Harvey asked.

"Thirteen," Lukie replied. "She's the only dog I've ever had."

"It's hard, losing your dog. After my mother passed away, my dad got me a little beagle, but it got convulsions and died. It's very hard."

"Dr. Bortman over at the animal hospital says you should always be prepared to outlive your dog," Lukie said. "He's going to give me a puppy when Lady dies, but I don't think I'll ever want another dog."

"You should get one, though," Harvey said. "It's like being thrown from a horse — you're supposed to climb right back on."

"Is that what you did, get another dog?"

"No," Harvey admitted. "I was tired of everyone's dying on me."

As Christmas approached, Main Street was crowded with shoppers, and the merchants took on extra help for the holiday rush. Billy and Junior formed a partnership and sold Christmas trees in an empty lot next to Selma's Dress Shop. Sally was hired to work Friday nights and Saturdays at the D & C dime store. Lukie, meantime, landed a permanent part-time job at the *Clarion* — reading proof and running errands. The girls were glad to have the work; they needed money for the cottage they

65

were going to rent up at Clam Lake in the summer.

Harvey's little dance band was in great demand for holiday parties — at the Elks Club and Legion Hall and the Knights of Columbus. Two nights before Christmas, however, he found time to take Lukie to the show again. He seemed melancholy and distracted. All through the movie he twisted restlessly in his seat and kept removing his glasses and rubbing his eyes. Lukie had noticed he was given to shifting moods. Musicians were inclined toward temperament, she had heard; perhaps that was true of Harvey.

When the show let out, there was a little disagreement over where they should go.

"The Sweet Shoppe?" Lukie suggested. "Or Crissman's soda fountain? Or we could just take a walk."

"A walk?" Harvey said irritably. "Is that your idea of fun?"

"You don't have to be so crabby about it, Harvey," Lukie replied, her feelings hurt.

"Well, it seems that's all anybody does in this town," Harvey complained; "take a walk or go to the Sweet Shoppe. I mean, in Ann Arbor there's something doing every night of the week — plays and concerts and dances."

"Zebron Falls isn't Ann Arbor, Harvey," Lukie said curtly.

In the end, they split an order of French fries at the Sweet Shoppe. Harvey apologized to Lukie for snapping at her.

"It's just Christmas, I guess," he said. "Christmas always makes me feel sort of blue. I mean, we've moved around so much, my dad and I, that we've never had a real home."

"How many towns did you live in before you came to Zebron Falls?"

"Four."

"Well," Lukie said softly, "you've got a home now, don't you?"

Harvey didn't answer. A Benny Goodman number was playing on the jukebox, and he had become engrossed in drawing the mathematical scheme of the arrangement on a paper napkin.

"See the progression?" He showed the napkin to Lukie. "Two, four, eight, and then, in the last bar, eight, four, two. If it won't work mathematically, it won't work musically."

Lukie didn't understand a bit of it, but she was glad Harvey's spirits had improved, and on the way home, she sneaked up behind him and stuffed snow down his collar — which touched off a running snowball fight, through the cemetery and out Old Perch Road, the night cold and clear and the snow squeaking underfoot. As they leaped up on the front porch, laughing and out of breath, Harvey suddenly pulled Lukie to him and kissed her on the mouth. It was a quick kiss, shy and sweetly awkward, and their noses bumped.

"Good night, Harvey," Lukie whispered. "I had a lovely time."

She floated up the back stairway, aglow with excitement. She had a boyfriend, she thought as she undressed in the dark. There would be dances and parties and double dates with Junior and Sally. And Billy. No,

67

not Billy — after all, there *were* the limits.

She felt a twinge of guilt, as if she had somehow betrayed their friendship. Quickly, she went to the desk, switched the gooseneck lamp on and off, then looked out the dormer window toward Great Oaks and waited. There was no response. Billy was probably already in bed, she thought, but he still might have seen them on the porch. She bit her lip and crawled into bed. She hoped he hadn't — but didn't understand why.

11

In January, Lukie's duties at the *Clarion* were expanded to include proofing the classified pages and maintaining the circulation files. She shared an old rolltop desk with Mrs. LaBurge, a deep-bosomed, self-important woman, whose disfavor Lukie quickly incurred by innocently using the wrong desk drawer for her copy pencils.

"I'd watch my p's and q's, if I were you, young lady," Mrs. LaBurge snapped, throwing Lukie's things on the floor. "This isn't the Tuesday Musicale."

But aside from having to endure Beatrice LaBurge's haughty disposition, Lukie liked working in the dusty little *Clarion* office. She liked the special newspaper smells of mucilage and printer's ink and hot lead. And she liked Mr. Seed, a gruff but patient editor, who ran the paper as much from the first stool at Van's 406 Bar as from his desk.

"The primary purpose of a newspaper," he was fond of saying, "is to go to press. Be prompt, be neat, be concise."

Mr. Seed worked closely with Lukie for a few days, instructing her in typefaces and proofreader's symbols. Then one Monday he handed her a thick stack of galleys.

"Leave them on my desk when you're finished," he said. "I've got to cover the Road Commission meeting tonight, but I'll need them first thing in the morning."

As Mr. Seed left, Mrs. LaBurge was coming in to type up her column. Lukie tactfully took the proofs to a table in the back of the office and cleared herself a place to work. She triple-checked every line to make sure she'd caught all the errors, but when she came in the next afternoon Mr. Seed took her aside.

"Did you do those proofs yesterday?" he asked sternly.

"Yes, sir."

"We searched high and low and couldn't find them."

"But I put them on your desk," Lukie said, "just as you said."

"Did you spike them?"

"No, sir, but I weighted them down with a lead slug."

Mr. Seed shook his head and frowned.

"You'll have to be more careful, Lukie. It costs money to keep a press operator overtime. Always spike the proofs. Things get lost in the clutter."

That evening, Lukie stayed late at the paper. When Mrs. LaBurge and others had gone, she rummaged through the office, looking for the missing proofs. She was just about to give up when her eyes fell on Mrs. LaBurge's private drawer. Slowly, she pulled the drawer open. The proofs were wadded up under some old advertising mats. Lukie sank into a chair in disbelief.

"But how could she!" she said aloud.

After that, Lukie made it a point to submit her proofs personally to Mr. Seed, and he seemed pleased with her work. One day, when he was "indisposed" at Van's 406, he left word that Lukie was to pick up ad copy from the merchants. She felt very important as she made her rounds, checking ad layouts and listening to the complaints about business. She stopped at George Becker's Barber Shop last. The place was warm and cozy, and filled with the sweet smell of bay rum and hair tonic.

"Good afternoon, Lukie." Mr. Becker smiled. "Be with you in a minute."

Lukie sat in one of the polished chairs near the window, watching the shoppers outside hurry up Main Street in the snow. The soft barber shop sounds of snipping and combing and brushing made her drowsy. She closed her eyes and eavesdropped on the conversations around her. The man in Mr. Becker's chair was talking about the new war contract that Higbie Manufacturing had been awarded. The firm would have to expand its facilities, he said, and there was concern that the new jobs might attract a lot of hillbillies and niggers. That's what had happened in Detroit, the man said. Thousands of them had come up from the South for jobs in the war plants, and one day there would be trouble. The hillbillies weren't so bad, but the niggers would ruin everything. They would want to live next door to you and marry your daughter.

As Lukie listened, her eyes came open, and she felt a tightening in her stomach. She looked over at the door, half-expecting to see Billy or his father walk in — and then she remembered that Mrs. Butts cut their hair at home. They never went to the barber shop; it was one of the limits.

The episode made Lukie look at Billy's situation in a new light. It seemed that the older he got, the more complicated his life became. It was only half a life, she was beginning to realize, for so much was shut off to him — no dates, no dances, no sweet moments of discovery up on Squirrel Road.

She remembered when she was a little girl and was taken to the big hospital in Pontiac to have her tonsils removed. She had been one of a large group of children who were there for the same purpose. One of the boys was colored. When the nurse instructed them to line up in twos, Lukie had instinctively taken the colored boy by the hand. "It was so sweet!" her mother told people afterward. "She didn't want the boy to feel left out." But it hadn't been anything of the sort. She had simply assumed that since the boy was a Negro, he was a friend of Billy's and would look after her.

Lukie was aware of the mean side of Zebron Falls. Tom Howlett, the chief of police, fixed tickets for his friends, and certain merchants had a private agreement not to undersell each other. Mrs. Higbie drank so much she saw snakes, and the volunteer firemen showed dirty movies at their smokers in the back of Eddie Spilak's bump shop. There was gossip and backbiting and pettiness, and if you were a Catholic you got blackballed at the Elks Club.

But Lukie had always accepted the mean things simply

as being part of human nature. What was important was the oneness of the town. People knew when you were born and cared when you died. Dr. Geist brought you into the world and came in the night when you were sick. You grew up and went to Zebron High and got a job at Higbie's or the mill. You raised a family and sat on the porch on warm summer nights, and then when your time came, Mr. Potere, at the funeral home, a pleasant man whose grief was real, took you to the cemetery. Lukie couldn't imagine a nicer way of life. You knew your place and felt your worth. Now, however, she wondered. Was Zebron Falls that way for Billy?

February came in with a massive blizzard that shut down Higbie's and the mill for two days. When the weather cleared, Billy came by to see Lukie just as her seventh-hour chemistry lab was letting out.

"Sharpen your skates, ol' buddy," he said. "We're going to skate up the river."

"When?" Lukie asked eagerly.

"Saturday, after supper."

"In the dark?"

"There'll be less wind. We're going to try to top your Uncle Farnie's record."

Lukie's eyes lit up. "Twenty bridges?"

"Twenty-one," Billy corrected her. "We'll need twenty just to tie."

On Saturday, Mr. Seed kept Lukie late at the *Clarion*, getting out subscription notices. When she got home, she bolted her supper, then ran upstairs to get ready. Something was bothering Billy, she thought as she pulled a pair of leggings on under her heaviest wool skirt; she

73

could always tell. Perhaps he would talk about it tonight.

"You won't be late, will you, dear?" Myrene Bishop asked as Lukie hurried down to the kitchen.

"There's no telling, Mama. Uncle Farnie holds the record — twenty bridges. We're going to try to break it."

Myrene Bishop looked up sharply from the sink.

"Where on earth did you hear that?"

Lukie grabbed a handful of stove matches from the cupboard and stuffed them in the pocket of her coat. It was the new winter coat her mother had made for her out of blanket material — navy blue, with brass buttons and gold satin lining, extra-heavy so that the wool wouldn't prick through.

"Hear what, Mama?" she said distractedly.

"About your Uncle Farnsworth skating twenty bridges?"

"He told me himself. Why?"

"Oh-h, no reason," her mother replied vaguely. "I hadn't realized he still held the record, that's all."

A shrill whistle sounded from outside. Lukie ran to the big bay window in the dining room. Billy was coming up the frozen driveway, his skates tied around his neck. Lukie rapped on the windowpane and waved.

"I'm coming, Billy!" she called. "I'm coming!"

12

They glided under the Gunn Road bridge, then curved smoothly around a bend in the snow-banked river. The night was cold but clear and dry, and the runners of their skates flashed in the moonlight. They were both in fine spirits, and when they came to a spot where the river widened and the ice was smooth as glass, they started showing off to one another. Billy skated around in a series of tight circles, his hands clasped behind his back and his body set in a low crouch, like a racer. Lukie, not to be outdone, executed a perfect figure eight, followed by a little pirouette — which ended with her sprawled ungracefully on the ice. Billy helped her to her feet and dusted the snow from her coat.

"How are your ankles holding out?" he asked.

"Fine," Lukie replied breathlessly. "I feel as if I could skate all night."

They started back up the river. The night was quiet, except for the whisper of their skates on the ice. Lights glowed from a distant farmhouse. Lukie had a pleasant feeling of isolation. Winter hung heavy over a town, but it was different in the country.

"Let's do thirty bridges, Billy," she said excitedly. "Let's set a record that will stand forever."

But in the end, Uncle Farnie's record remained secure. A half-mile above the fifteenth bridge, the river became almost impassable. There were deep snow drifts, and fishing holes where the ice was dangerously thin. They decided to give it up.

"And we were doing so well!" Lukie pouted.

"Come on," Billy said, skating in toward shore, "let's warm our bones before we start back."

In order to find dry kindling for a fire, they had to climb to a wooded slope in the bluffs above the river. Billy collected the kindling. Lukie broke off some evergreen boughs and made a matting for them in the snow. The fire blazed up quickly, and as they warmed themselves, Billy began to talk.

His father had given him two axioms, he said. The first was that when you're in a minority, you've got to run twice as fast as the others just to stay in place. The second one was, simply, don't be pushy.

"And so I've joined the Army. I'll be called up the day after my eighteenth birthday."

Lukie was dumfounded.

"But what about Ann Arbor, Billy?"

"It will just have to wait. A lot of things will have to wait."

"But your birthday is the first week of May. What about graduation?"

"That's part of the problem."

He had learned from Mr. Severence that he was going to be valedictorian of his class, Billy said. Even though commencement was over three months away, his average was so far above the others, it was unlikely that anyone would catch up to him. And being valedictorian was fine — it fit in with his father's first axiom. But it meant giving the valedictory at commencement, and that wasn't so fine. He had been captain of the football team and president of the Student Council. He had been everything there was to be at Zebron High, and that had helped him stay in place. But the valedictory would be pushy. It would be resented — not by the kids but by the parents, which was worse. He had discussed the matter with his father and with Mr. Severence. He would be permitted to take his exams early. By commencement day, he would be safely tucked away at Fort Sheridan, doing close-order drill, or something.

Lukie felt a great sadness well up in her.

"Is that the only reason you're doing it, Billy?" she asked. "To get out of commencement?"

"No," Billy replied. "It just simplifies things. I'd made up my mind to do it regardless. I've got to keep up the pace."

And then he broke into a grin.

"Besides, I might get stationed out East, and my Uncle Zeke says a guy ought to see Harlem before he settles down. 'Live a little, Billy boy,' he keeps telling me. 'Savor the tinkling glasses and the silken ladies.' "

They fell into silence. There seemed to be nothing more to say. The fire died down. A train whistle wailed mournfully from the direction of town. Billy got to his feet.

"That's probably the ten–fifty-five from Detroit," he said. "We'd better start back."

Lukie sighed. "It's funny, isn't it, how growing up creeps up on you?"

As they started back down to the river, there occurred a timeless moment that Lukie knew she would always hold in her heart. From the edge of the bluff, there was a perfect view of Zebron Falls, nestled in the valley in the moonlight — the rooftops, the church spires, the twinkling lights — as if sketched on an artist's canvas. It all seemed so lovely, so indestructible. She thought of *Jane Eyre*, which she had been reading for her course in the Victorian novelists. She had been deeply influenced by the book and had come to believe, as did Jane, in an invisible world of spirits commissioned to guard over the living. And as she stood on the bluff and looked down over the town, it was as if she could sense the presence of all who had gone before her — in this land, on this river, far back to Joshua Zebron and the early settlers, and to the Ottawa and Huron tribes before them — invisible sentinels watching over the town, on and on and on, in the sweetness of spring, in the haze of an autumn evening, in the hush of a first snowfall — everlastingly, never-endingly. And she was convinced that no matter where Billy went or what he did, these spirits of the past would protect him and bring him home safe, until it was time for him, too — for all of them — to pass into the invisible kingdom that was their destiny.

And then she felt Billy take her hand.

"Are you ready, Lukie?"

"Yes, Billy, I'm ready."

Billy Butts left Zebron Falls on a glistening morning in May, on the 5:35 milk train to Detroit. The long, hard winter had produced a breathtakingly beautiful spring. The daffodils were out, and the golden forsythia seemed to glow in the gathering dawn. A sleepy-eyed crowd was waiting at the depot to see Billy off. Junior Rosenquist was choked with emotion.

"So long, sport," he said, giving Billy a little bear hug.

"So long, Junior."

"I'm cooking up a little scheme, so get the Army all shaped up, huh, sport? I'll be along soon."

"Sure you will, Junior." Billy grinned. "Sure you will."

Miss Pray, her hair still in curlers, showed up just as the train was pulling out. She ran down the platform, waving.

"Do us proud, Billy!" she called above the rumble of the locomotive. "Do your town proud!"

The train went out of sight down the tracks. Lukie turned to Junior.

"Oh, Junior, what are we going to do without Billy?" she said sadly. "He held everything together."

With Billy gone, Lukie became listless and withdrawn. She spent most of her spare time in her vegetable garden or at her place above the river. She saw Harvey occasionally, but she lacked the energy to cope with his erratic moods and his esoteric musical interests. It wasn't until Billy's first letter arrived — full of confidence and cheer

79

and funny remarks about the Army — that she finally pulled herself together and began to pick up her life, and even then the fun seemed to have gone out of everything. It was as if she had lost not merely her best friend but her — no, she wouldn't even let herself think it.

13

And then on a bright day in June — school was out. A roar of elation filled the halls of Zebron High. Lockers were hastily cleaned out, forgotten gym equipment was turned in, goodbyes were said to vacationing teachers.

For two years, Miss Pray had been planning a Caribbean cruise to Trinidad and the Bahamas, but German submarines were still operating freely in coastal waters — a fact that made her available to chaperone Lukie and Sally at their rented cottage up at Clam Lake.

It was a pretty, green-shuttered cottage, across the lake from an old casino, with a screened-in porch and a boathouse. A path led back through a grove of hemlock trees to an outhouse with a half-moon carved in the door. Sally puzzled over a coffee can, filled with a white, powdery substance, that sat on a ledge in the outhouse.

"It's lime," explained Lukie, who had had experience

with such things at her Grandpa Axford's cabin up on the Au Sable River. "You're supposed to sprinkle it down the hole after you go."

"But what if something crawls up and bites you?" Sally grimaced.

Lukie laughed herself silly.

The week seemed to fly by. There were languid afternoons spent on the beach or in the shade of the hemlocks, reading. At night, cars filled with laughing couples from Zebron Falls pulled noisily in and out of the driveway, and there was dancing out on the pier.

Harvey came up the first night, nervous about his band's forthcoming opening at Ollie Trout's.

"What if we flop?" He brooded most of the evening.

Junior was busy at home, preparing to leave with his mother for the family's summer place up in Harbor Springs, but he had promised Sally he would stop by before they left — with a "big surprise," he hinted mysteriously.

"He's up to something," Sally said, worried. "I can tell."

In the mornings, there were long, lazy breakfasts, followed by gabfests with Miss Pray, who amazed Lukie with her breadth of knowledge. She rambled on in a thought-provoking series of aphorisms. Science confirmed religion. Newton's first law of physics had a moral application. All ages see through a glass darkly, and who was to say what lay beyond the grave? One morning, she reminisced about her Bohemian days in Chicago — about the artists and poets and radicals and the crazy things they did.

"What's a Bohemian, anyway?" Sally asked.

"A Bohemian is — well, it's a frame of mind, Sally," Miss Pray explained. "A transition, I suppose you'd call it. You question the old ways and think up grand schemes to reform the world. But the world can stand only so much reforming, and so you gradually come to accept the necessity of things. But not entirely, and to the extent that you reject the old ways, the old ideas — well, that's what keeps the world changing from generation to generation."

As Lukie listened, she thought how satisfying it must be to pursue deep scholarly interests. She pictured herself at the university, studying the Greek philosophers, and Cicero in the original Latin. And the great composers, too, for she was lost whenever Harvey discussed his music. She tried to express her feelings to him when they went out on the lake one evening, but he seemed impatient with her, and his eyes were bothering him.

"I probably need new glasses again," he complained, squinting. "It's the third time this year."

Lukie rowed them out to the middle of the lake, then let the boat drift. Harvey sat in the wide rear seat, absorbed in a new arrangement he was working on for the band.

"Harvey," Lukie asked idly, "who wrote the Fifth Symphony?"

"Every composer that wrote more than four," Harvey answered, without looking up.

It took Lukie a moment to realize she had been belittled.

"Harvey, I just can't figure you out!" she said irritably.

"Sometimes you're so — sar*don*ic! Music isn't the only thing in the world, you know. I mean, can you force-bloom azaleas or do a cleft graft on an apple tree?"

Harvey drew a deep breath and put aside his music.

"I'm sorry," he said wearily, rubbing his eyes. "It's just my heebie-jeebies."

"Your what?" Lukie said, wrinkling her brow.

"Nerves," Harvey said, embarrassed. "Funny things happen to me whenever I'm going to play somewhere. I get palpitations and keep thinking I'll die or hurt my hands before the performance begins."

"You should see Dr. Geist," Lukie said, concern showing in her eyes. "It might be something serious."

"What for?" Harvey shrugged. "It goes away as soon as I start playing, and then I'm fine." He lowered his eyes. "Look, it's hard to explain. Why don't you come by the news agency when you get back to town? There's something I want to show you."

"All right," Lukie agreed, somewhat mollified. "But you still haven't answered my question."

"Beethoven's is the most famous, and then Tchaikovsky's. Miss Pray has a big volume at the library that lists all the composers."

"Thank you, Harvey." Lukie smiled, softening. "You're a very nice boy."

"Do you really mean that?"

"Of course I do."

"Gee, thanks." Harvey grinned. "You're pretty swell, yourself."

Lukie could seldom stay mad at Harvey for long. There was so much to like about him: his intensity, his quick mind, his sly sense of humor. Sometimes he kept them all in stitches doing funny routines on the piano at Tuesday Musicale. He was a cut above the other boys — even Junior — with a kind of unpretentious refinement that he had probably acquired from his father. He opened doors and held your coat, and he nearly always noticed your clothes and had a nice comment. When he wasn't in a cloud of preoccupation over his music, he liked to listen to Lukie talk — about herself and her family and Zebron Falls. It was as if he were trying to share her roots, and at those times he made her feel like the most important person on earth.

"Well," Harvey said, gathering up his notes, "I guess we'd better start back."

The sun had gone down. The sounds of music and gaiety drifted out from the casino. Impulsively, Lukie moved to the rear of the boat and slipped into Harvey's arms.

"Kiss me, Harvey," she whispered. "No — kiss me our special way."

On Friday night, Lukie and Sally and Miss Pray rowed down to the little resort village at the foot of the lake for the opening of "Harvey Toles and the Aristocrats" at Ollie Trout's. Lukie had never been to a roadhouse before. The place was dim and smoky. Purple lights played over the dance floor. Lukie felt very grown up.

"I can hardly hear myself think!" she called above the music to Miss Pray and Sally. And she laughed.

They had a fine time. Miss Pray ordered a sloe gin fizz for herself and treated Sally and Lukie to Cokes and French-fried shrimp. The band was a huge success.

Harvey had brought his violin, and did a "jazz fiddle" rendition of "Ain't Misbehavin' " that brought down the house. It was the first time Lukie had heard him play the violin, and she was awed by his talent.

"And to think," Miss Pray said as she beamed, "he's one of our very own Tuesday Musicale youngsters!"

It was nearly midnight when they started back up the lake to the cottage. It was Sally's turn to row, and when she maneuvered the boat in toward shore, they all noticed a shadowy figure standing on the pier. It was Junior. He had come up on the train while they were at Ollie Trout's, and now he had missed that last train back and was stuck.

"Can he stay at the cottage tonight, Miss Pray?" Sally asked anxiously. "Please?"

"This modern generation!" Miss Pray sighed. "Get him some blankets, Sally. There's an old mattress out in the boathouse. He can sleep there, and then after breakfast we'll row him down to the depot."

Miss Pray went straight to bed. Lukie and Sally got out the spare bedding they'd brought along for just such a contingency.

"All right," Sally said to Junior as they walked down to the boathouse, "what's the big surprise?"

"It's still confidential," Junior said evasively. "Let's just say the next time you see me there might be a change in my status."

"Junior Rosenquist!" Sally demanded. "What have you got up your sleeve?"

"Okay, okay — but mum's the word, understand?"

He had figured out a way to enlist underage in the

Army, he told them. He was going to register for the draft up in Harbor Springs — at the county seat, where nobody knew him — and use his family's summer home as an address. If he pulled it off, he planned to volunteer for immediate induction, which meant he would be called up within thirty days.

"Oh, honestly, Junior!" Sally said, in tears. "You boys are such dumb — patriots. Wouldn't it be enough just to do your duty when the time comes, without running off before you've even graduated?"

"I'm going to catch up to Billy," Junior said firmly. "We're going to be a team again."

"But, Junior," Sally argued, "there's no guarantee you'd be assigned to Billy's unit."

"Oh, yeah?" Junior winked. "My old man knows a three-star general in Washington."

Lukie said, "We could squeal on you, you know."

"You could," Junior agreed, "but you won't."

Sally fixed Junior a bed in the boathouse, and then she and Lukie started up to the cottage.

"All I ever wanted him to do," Sally said, "was stand on his own two feet, but this is crazy."

An outboard motor droned in the night. A cool breeze was blowing up off the lake. Lukie had the feeling their week at Clam Lake was about to end on a sour note. Suddenly, Sally turned back toward the boathouse.

"I'm going to sit with him for a while," she said. "Maybe he'll listen to reason."

Two days later, tired and sunburned, the girls packed their blankets and souvenirs into Miss Pray's Nash coupe, and the three of them started for home.

87

"Aren't vacations ex*hau*sting?" Sally remarked.

As they drove through the village, Lukie asked Miss Pray to stop at the post office, which was in the general store. She had written a postcard to Billy, and wanted it to have a Clam Lake postmark.

Dear Billy,
I hooked a fine walleye and bought a funny hat at a curio shop. Harvey's band was a big hit at Ollie Trout's. Sally's nose is peeling (on her it looks good!). Don't breathe a word, but Junior is determined to join the Army — more on that later. Everybody asks about you. Write!!!

Love and kisses,
Your ol' buddy, Lukie

14

He's coming home!"

Lukie, waving a letter, burst into the Sweet Shoppe — barefoot, in shorts and a halter, and with her tanned legs still dusty from the garden.

"Billy's coming home!"

She slid into the booth where Sally and Lorena Pearsall and Addison Carey were spooning caramel sundaes.

"When?" Sally asked eagerly.

"Next Monday," Lukie replied, handing Sally the letter. "For a week."

"How wonderful!" Sally cried. "Maybe we could all go up to Harbor Springs and see Junior."

The letter was postmarked Maxwell Field, an Army Air Corps base in Alabama. He was there for training in radio and radar, Billy had written, after which he would probably be assigned to a B-17 crew. He was being given a furlough before classes commenced and would arrive in

Zebron Falls Monday morning, on the 10:15 local from Detroit.

"Let's throw a party for him!" Sally suggested.

"Where?" Lukie asked.

"At my house," Addison Carey put in. "We just got a new automatic phonograph. Lorena, bring your Tommy Dorsey records."

Lukie worked hurriedly to get her vegetable garden in order, so that it would require a minimum of attention while Billy was home. They would take a picnic lunch to their spot on the river, she decided, and fish and swim and doze in the shade. Harvey's band would be playing at Ollie Trout's every night except Monday, so there would be no claims on her time.

One afternoon, she looked up from her gardening and was surprised to see her father coming down from the house. He was home early. There had been labor trouble at the mill, and he looked hot and tired.

"Your garden looks fine," he called to her. "Are the squash bugs bad this year?"

"Not too bad, Daddy." Lukie pushed back her straw hat and wiped the beads of perspiration from her brow. "I rinsed the plants in soap and water. It helps."

She started out of the garden, searching her father's face for the cross look that always preceded a reprimand, but he seemed in a pleasant mood.

"Your mother wants to know what you'd like to serve for dinner when Billy comes over."

"Leg of lamb," Lukie answered. "Billy said he's dying for a good leg of lamb, with mashed potatoes and gravy and cherry pie."

At the end of the garden was a trellised grape arbor with two little wooden benches. Lukie curled up on one of the benches and fanned herself with her hat.

"Is there going to be a strike at the mill, Daddy," she asked, "the way everybody says?"

"No," her father replied, "but the union will get in. Which is fine, but I regret the necessity of it. People are inclined to act hostilely when they deal with each other through organizations. They do things they wouldn't do as individuals. But — times are changing."

They chatted for half an hour. It was the first time her father had held a real conversation with her since — Lukie couldn't remember when.

"You'll be starting your senior year soon," Walter Bishop said. "Have you thought about college?"

"Yes, but I really haven't decided yet."

"Think seriously about it," her father advised. "A girl should have something to fall back on — teaching or nursing, something like that."

He started to leave, then turned back.

"By the way, have you seen your Uncle Farnie lately? I hear he doesn't look too well."

"No sir, he doesn't," Lukie replied. "But it's hard to tell whether it's from being sick or just from the tap room."

"Yes." Walter Bishop frowned. "That was always Farnie's one great flaw."

"Even in the war?"

"No, he was fine in the war. It wasn't until after he got home. But — he had his reasons."

That night, Myrene Bishop came up to Lukie's room.

"Will your green beans be in by the time Billy gets home, dear?"

"No, Mama, but my spinach will. Billy's very fond of spinach."

She told her mother about the conversation with her father.

"Yes." Myrene Bishop nodded. "I've had the feeling that he's slowly moving toward a reconciliation with your Uncle Farnie. It's because of you, you know."

"Me? What did I do?"

"Oh, you've been a link; you've kept him informed. He admires the way you keep traipsing off to Uncle Farnie's place, in spite of everything."

"Did he really say that?"

"Oh, your father says many complimentary things behind your back."

"Well, for Pete's sake, Mama," Lukie said impatiently, "why doesn't he say a few of them to my face? I mean, it might just improve the morale around here."

"Don't get on your high horse, dear. Your father finds it hard to say what's in him."

Lukie studied her mother for a moment.

"Mama, what really happened between Daddy and Uncle Farnie?" she asked. "I know there are things you haven't told me."

"Oh, it was nothing, really," Myrene Bishop replied lightly. "Just some silly argument over the orchard. Your father thought it should have been sold off with the rest of the land, but Farnsworth refused."

"Uncle Farnie owns the orchard?" Lukie said, wide-eyed. "I thought it was ours."

"No, it's the last of Farnsworth's share of the estate. I don't know why he's hung on to it all these years. I suppose he sees it as a remnant of the past."

"The *last* of his share?" Lukie looked puzzled. "Was there more?"

Myrene Bishop sat down on the edge of the bed and sighed deeply.

"Well — I suppose you're old enough to know," she began. "It was shortly after your father and I were married. Farnsworth drank up the money for Grandpa Bishop's insurance premium, and your grandfather died before anyone discovered it."

"Oh, my gosh!" Lukie gasped.

"And so the farm was saddled with debts," her mother continued, "and the insurance had lapsed. Farnsworth did his best to make up for it. He signed his share of the estate over to your father, except for the orchard, but it wasn't much help. The immediate need was ready cash to hold off the creditors."

"What did Daddy do?" Lukie asked.

"What your father always does, dear," her mother said with a smile. "He stuck it out. He was a senior at the university then, and I was teaching art over in Pontiac. Between the two of us, we managed to keep things afloat for a while. But then you came along, and your father dropped out of college and went to work at the mill. It was a great disappointment to him. He has always regretted not getting his degree . . ."

And suddenly her father's resentment of her became clear to Lukie. She had been a mistake, an interference in his career.

"So that's it," she said tightly. "I was a complication."

"Lukie!" Her mother glared. "Don't talk like that! You were a responsibility, that's all. We were both responsibilities, and your father is a very responsible man."

But Lukie wasn't listening. She was imagining how it must have been when she was a baby, her father looking into her crib and seeing not a daughter but — an albatross. He probably didn't even pass out cigars. Well, she would be out of his life soon enough . . .

"No wonder he's so anxious to pack me off to college," Lukie said. "So he won't have to stare at me across the table."

"Now you listen to me, young lady!" Myrene Bishop grabbed her daughter by the shoulders and shook her hard. "It's time you stopped sitting in judgment on the world! Wallowing in self-pity isn't going to improve matters with your father. It's going to take effort, real effort!"

"But I've tried, Mama!" Lukie cried. "I've tried!"

"Have you? You avoid him like the plague and turn the other way whenever he comes into the room. You've become a mystery to him."

And then she gathered Lukie into her arms and began stroking her hair.

"I'm sorry to scold you, dear, but you're going to have to go halfway with him, perhaps more. When you were a little girl you used to hide in the bittersweet till you saw him coming home from work and then race out to greet him. Whatever happened to that little girl?"

The memory came back to Lukie with vivid clarity. He

would sweep her up into his arms and pretend she'd startled him.

"All right, Mama." Lukie sighed. "I'll try harder."

"Promise?"

Lukie looked up at her mother and smiled.

"Promise."

15

Lukie took an immediate liking to Harvey's father. Ira Toles was a thin, sad-eyed man with a gentle manner and a fine sense of humor. He wore an old tweed jacket with leather-patched elbows, even though the day was warm, and Lukie wondered if he was susceptible to chills. Harvey had told her that he read deep books and could quote from the classics.

"The weird one is up in his inner sanctum," Mr. Toles said the afternoon Lukie dropped by the news agency.

"The weird one?" Lukie puzzled.

"You mean he's been concealing his eccentricities from you?" Ira Toles asked, feigning surprise. "A boy has to be weird to spend such a lovely summer day practicing a Chopin sonata." Then he smiled and threw up his hands. "But — such is the life of a virtuoso."

Lukie laughed.

"Tell me, how is your father? I sit next to him at the Businessman's Association, you know."

"Really?"

"Oh, yes." Mr. Toles nodded. "He's a fine man. Tell him hello."

He motioned to a door behind the magazine racks.

"You might as well run on up," he said. "The virtuoso is expecting you."

The door opened on a stairway that led up to the living quarters, which consisted of three rooms and a kitchen. The place looked cozy and comfortable, and Lukie had the feeling no one would mind if she put her feet up on the couch.

"Welcome to our garret!" Harvey called from the doorway of his bedroom. "Come on in. I was just cataloging some stuff."

Lukie stopped short as she entered the room. She could barely see the furniture for all the books and musical scores, great stacks of them, on the chairs, on the floor, even on the windowsill.

"Is this what you wanted to show me?" she asked.

"Yes."

She gasped. "My gosh, Harvey, how do you manage to breathe?"

"Would you believe I know where everything is?" Harvey said proudly.

It seemed to Lukie that all the music in the world was crammed into the small, low-ceilinged bedroom — symphonies and sonatas, concertos and fugues.

"The great composers felt things in a very special way," Harvey said, "and when you play their music exactly as they conceived it, their feelings become yours, too. I can't do it yet, but I'm getting close."

Lukie browsed through one of the stacks, glancing at the titles — "Havanaise," "Scottish Fantasy," "Concerto in D Major."

"This was the first item in my collection," Harvey said, tossing her a yellowed book of violin exercises. "My mother gave it to me when I was four years old. She was a music teacher."

"How old were you when she died?" Lukie asked.

"Eight."

"Do you remember much about her?"

"Everything — but especially the music lessons," Harvey said, sitting cross-legged on the bed. "And her hair. It was like yours, long and straight, only brown instead of black."

He seemed oddly vulnerable, Lukie thought, in a rumpled white shirt and with his hair falling down over his eyes.

"There was a Chopin sonata my mother was very fond of," Harvey said shyly. "Whenever I play it I get the feeling she's with me. Does that sound spooky?"

"No, Harvey, I think it's lovely."

Harvey talked for a long time that afternoon — about how his music absorbed all of his energies, how it constantly filled his mind and made him resentful of interruptions, how sometimes he hated it, for it set him apart from the other boys. It was as if he realized his talent was also his weakness, Lukie thought, and was appealing for patience and understanding. Or maybe that wasn't it at all. Maybe he was trying to warn her.

It was nearly six o'clock when she got up to leave.

"Aren't you staying for supper?" Harvey asked.

"It depends." Lukie giggled. "Who does the cooking?"

"It's my turn tonight. I'm fixing pilaf. It's like a Bach fugue — it never comes out the same way twice."

It was a fine meal. Mr. Toles kept up a lively flow of conversation about literature and the arts, and Harvey kept jumping up and down to play little passages on the upright piano. For dessert, there were cherry tarts from the Home Bakery, served with rich black coffee in tiny cups. Mr. Toles lit candles and insisted that Harvey serenade Lukie on his violin. Afterward, the three of them pitched in on the dishes.

"I'm glad you came," Harvey said when Lukie was leaving.

"I'm glad, too, Harvey."

But, walking home, she was more confused than ever about her feelings for Harvey. One thing, however, was clear to her. Any girl that married Harvey Toles would be committing herself to a — vocation.

16

The day before Billy was due to arrive home, a mass of hot, humid air moved in from the southwest and hung oppressively over the valley. The temperature rose into the nineties, and there was barely a whisper of breeze. No relief was forecast till Monday night at the earliest.

That afternoon, Lukie and Sally went to the matinee at the Hills Theater to see *The Song of Bernadette*. When Lukie got home, her mother and father were huddled anxiously around the radio in the sunroom.

"What is it, Mama?" Lukie asked.

"Shhh!" Myrene Bishop put a finger to her lips. "There's been some trouble in Detroit — a race riot."

It had started in a municipal park, the man on the radio was saying, where thousands of people had thronged to escape the summer heat. Now, disturbances were spreading throughout the city. Negroes were being attacked wherever they could be found. There had been looting and burning. Many people had been killed and many more injured. The city was out of control, and there were reports of the Army's being called in.

Lukie thought of the conversation she had overheard that day in George Becker's Barber Shop — and then she thought of Billy. He would be passing through Detroit tomorrow.

"Do you think he'll be all right, Daddy?" she asked her father.

"Well, he'll have to change trains and go crosstown from Union Station to the Michigan Central Terminal," Walter Bishop replied. "But Billy knows how to take care of himself. If he takes a cab or a streetcar, he should be all right. I imagine the police will have things in hand by then, anyway."

But by the next morning, the situation in Detroit had grown worse, and there were rumors that the trouble was spreading into rural areas. A tense mood gripped Zebron Falls. Case's Hardware was doing a brisk business in shotguns, and Tom Howlett, the chief of police, issued orders that any Negroes observed driving through town were to be stopped and searched and brought to the station for investigation.

Shortly after breakfast, Billy's father came over to see Lukie.

"Ella and I won't be going to the depot," he told her. "There are a few things we have to tend to. Billy will understand."

"It isn't fair!" Lukie complained to her mother. "Mr. Butts is one of the finest men in Zebron Falls. Why should he have to stay off the streets?"

"He knows what he's doing, dear," Myrene Bishop remarked. "Henry Butts has an unfailing sense of discretion."

At ten o'clock, a little crowd gathered at the depot, with signs and flags and noise-makers, to welcome Billy home — Lukie and Sally, Miss Pray and Mr. Panella, Lorena Pearsall and Addison Carey, even Harvey, who had canceled his appointment at the optometrist's just to be there. But when the 10:15 pulled in, Billy wasn't on it; nor was he on the next two trains. By one o'clock, storm clouds were gathering in the west, and the crowd gradually drifted off.

"Now, now, don't you worry," Miss Pray assured Lukie. "His furlough was probably canceled, or maybe he couldn't get a seat on the train from Alabama. I'm sure he'll phone or send a wire."

Lukie stayed at the depot for the rest of the day, meeting every train. Sally sat with her until supper time and then left.

"I'm supposed to baby-sit at the Whatelys' tonight," she said. "If I can get out of it, I'll come back."

"It's all right, Sally. At least one of us will be here if he comes in."

At dusk, the heat wave broke in a violent downpour. Lukie took shelter in the waiting room. Mr. Biggers, the stationmaster, came out from the ticket office and offered to have the porter drive her home.

"There's no point in sitting here all night, Lukie," he said. "I'll call the house if Billy shows up."

The rain was abating, and the sky was beginning to clear.

"All right," Lukie agreed. "After the eight–o-five comes in."

Billy was aboard the 8:05. It was growing dark, but she could make out a khaki-clad figure, with a duffel bag, climbing down from the last car. She raced up the platform.

"Billy!" she called as she waved.

And then she stopped abruptly. Billy's jaunty self-confidence seemed gone. His uniform was torn and stained, and there were ugly red welts on his face.

"Oh, Billy!" She gasped. "What have they done to you!"

But before Billy had a chance to answer, a tall, uniformed figure moved out of the shadows and pinned his arms behind his back. It was Tom Howlett.

"All right, soldier," he barked, "let's see what you've got in that bag."

"Mr. Howlett!" Lukie screamed in outrage. "It's Billy!"

Tom Howlett's mouth fell open. He relaxed his grip. Billy turned to face him.

"Billy . . ." he mumbled. "I didn't know. The trouble in Detroit — folks have been nervous — you know how it is."

"Yeah, Tom," Billy said, tight-lipped. "I know how it is."

"Well — it's good to have you home, Billy." Chief Howlett smiled but looked embarrassed. "Drop by the station before you leave. The boys still talk about the championship game."

He turned and hurried down the platform. Lukie put a hand on Billy's shoulder.

"He didn't mean it, Billy," she said softly.

Billy said nothing. He watched Tom Howlett drive off in his patrol car, then picked up his duffel bag and took Lukie's hand.

"Come on, ol' buddy," he said, walking purposefully toward the depot. "I've got things to do."

Inside the waiting room, Billy rapped on the ticket window.

"Could you write me a ticket to New York, Mr. Biggers?"

"New York?" said the stationmaster, befuddled. "My heavens, that was a quick visit, Billy."

"Yeah — well, something's come up. Route me through Sarnia instead of Detroit, okay?"

"It's a good bit longer, Billy."

"That's all right," Billy said. "When can I make a connection?"

"You're in luck." Mr. Biggers was consulting his gold railroad watch. "The Wolverine is due in six minutes."

Lukie watched Billy in disbelief.

"New *York*! Oh, Billy, you can't run off like this! Mama's going to have roast lamb, and I baked you a cherry pie!"

Billy took Lukie's arm and sat her down on one of the oak benches.

"Listen, Lukie," he said, "that letter about me going to be on a bomber crew? It was all a lie. Do you want to know what I am, Lukie? I'm a waiter — in the Officers' Club. And if I'm a good waiter, maybe one day they'll promote me to bartender. And if I don't like that, there's always the labor troops. You'd be amazed how many

104

ditches there are to be dug in the Army, Lukie, and latrines to be cleaned and potatoes to be peeled . . ."

"All right, so you're a waiter," Lukie said, in tears. "So what? At least that way maybe you'll stay alive. Oh, Billy, if you go away mad like this you'll get in trouble."

Billy sat down next to Lukie.

"Relax, Lukie." He nudged her. "I'm not mad. Just a little punch-drunk. Tom Howlett was sort of the last straw, that's all."

"But you know he didn't mean it, Billy."

"Yeah." Billy nodded. "But he meant it for *some*body, didn't he? Besides, I need to get my bearings, and Zebron Falls wouldn't be any good, not right now. It's not just Tom Howlett or what happened in Detroit today. I've been doing a lot of reading — Frederick Douglass and W. E. B. Du Bois and several of the African writers. Things have been kicking around in my mind, and — well, I've got to figure out how I fit into everything."

He laughed bitterly.

"The funny thing is, I always knew stuff like that existed — you know, sitting in the back of the bus and all that. But I never thought it would apply to me."

"I know," Lukie said, drying her eyes. "Neither did I."

A train whistle sounded in the distance.

"Do you want to tell me what happened in Detroit?" Lukie asked.

Billy shook his head.

"Maybe someday?"

"No," Billy said grimly, looking away from Lukie. "I don't ever want to tell anybody about that."

"Oh, Billy." Lukie sighed, leaning against his shoulder.

"I don't know how you put up with it. If Chief Howlett had done that to my father he would've had his badge in ten minutes."

"Yeah," Billy said derisively, "Tom was a regular G-man, wasn't he?"

"The town's been so ugly, Billy. Do you think what happened in Detroit could ever happen here?"

"Maybe," Billy answered, "but not if I have anything to say about it."

Bells clanged, and the gates started coming down over the Main Street crossing. Billy picked up his bag, and they went out onto the platform.

"Give my dad a call, will you? He'll understand."

"Will you go to Harlem while you're in New York?"

"Yeah. I guess I'll savor the tinkling glasses, like my Uncle Zeke said."

"You'd better change into a clean uniform," Lukie said, fussing with his tie. "You'll want to look nice for the silken ladies."

"Naw." Billy grinned now. "I've already savored them. They can't hold a candle to the home-grown variety."

"Really?" Lukie smiled.

"Yes, Lukie," Billy answered, looking deeply into her eyes. "Really."

And then their voices were lost in the roar of the train. Billy tossed his duffel bag up on the observation platform, then clambered aboard.

"Goodbye, Billy!" Lukie stood on her toes and clutched Billy's hand. "Take good care of yourself!"

She waved as the train rumbled up the tracks. For a

moment, as it curved into the woods above the village park, the observation car stood out vividly against the western sky. Lukie could see Billy waving. Even as a distant silhouette, she thought with pride, he looked special. She remembered the night they had skated up the river, the night she had felt the presence of invisible spirits guarding over the valley.

Wherever Billy was going, she felt sure, and whatever he was planning to do — people would know he had been there.

17

A week later, Junior Rosenquist, having successfully gotten himself drafted, slipped through Zebron Falls, en route to the military induction center in Detroit.

"Oh, Junior," Sally said tearfully, "why did you go and do it? You might get yourself killed!"

It was dusk of a hot day in July. Junior had popped out of the shadows in the orchard as Lukie and Sally were coming up from the river in their swimming suits.

"I've got to stay out of sight," he explained. "My dad thinks I'm up North with my mother, and she thinks I'm down here with him. It'll give me a head start."

"Where are you going to sleep tonight, Junior?" Lukie asked.

"I was hoping you'd let me stay in your garage, Lukie," Junior replied.

The garage had once been a barn, and the loft had

been fixed up as a sleeping room, with beds, already made up, and chairs and a washstand but no electricity. The girls took Junior up to the loft, then went up to the house and changed into their clothes. Lukie sneaked a plateful of ham sandwiches and a pitcher of milk from the kitchen, and the three of them sat out in the loft, talking in the dark, with the moonlight coming in the window and a breeze rustling in the trees.

"What about your folks, Junior?" Lukie asked. "They'll find out sooner or later."

"I'll send them a card," he said, "but I won't tell them where I am. It'll only be till September. I'll be legal after I turn seventeen."

He turned to Sally.

"I just had to get out from under my old man's thumb, Sally," he said, munching on a sandwich. "I mean, I love him and all that, but a guy's got to live his own life."

He had been feeling things deep in him that he wanted to express, he said, about Billy, about Zebron Falls. It had been that way ever since homecoming. Things just kept welling up in him, and he thought — well, he thought maybe he would become a writer.

"I'll talk it over with Billy," he said, reaching for another sandwich, "as soon as I catch up to him."

"It's no good, Junior," Sally said. "Even your father's big-shot friend in the War Department isn't going to get you assigned to Billy's unit."

"I don't understand . . ."

Sally looked at Lukie. "Tell him, Lukie," she said.

"Billy's a waiter, Junior," Lukie said, "at an Officers' Club down South."

Junior was speechless.

"The old sport a waiter?" he said finally. "A *wai*ter!"

"The rest of the world isn't like Zebron Falls, Junior. They give colored soldiers menial jobs and make them sit in the back of the bus."

The three of them sat in silence for several moments. Then Sally said, "It's not too late to get out of it, Junior. Just tell them at the induction center that you lied about your age. The most they'll probably do is give you a good scolding."

Junior squirmed restlessly in his chair.

"I can't, Sally. I've got my pride."

"Oh, honestly, Junior, you and your stupid pride!" Sally fumed. "You boys act as if the war was some great lark. Don't you care about me at all?"

"But it's you I'm thinking about, Sally. If I stick around, my old man will have me in a straitjacket. You don't know him the way I do. He's a hard man to stand up to. I've just got to make the break, with or without Billy, or I'll end up selling Studebakers for the rest of my life. Can't you see?"

Sally didn't say anything.

"Aw, come on, Sally, tell me it's okay."

"All right, Junior." Sally sighed resignedly. "Do whatever you think you have to do. I'll still be here."

In the morning, Lukie and Sally walked with Junior to the depot. He looked very forlorn, Lukie thought, as if wondering what the Army was going to be like without Billy.

He grinned nervously as the train pulled in. "Well, I

110

guess it'll be a while before I see the old home town again."

Sally went into Junior's arms and clung to him for a moment, and then Lukie hugged him.

"Goodbye, Junior," she whispered. "We all love you."

The girls watched the rickety milk train go out of sight. Then they turned and walked in silence through the empty streets of the town.

Homecoming, Lukie thought, seemed a thousand years ago.

Part Three

18

Then it was September, and Lukie wondered where the summer had gone. School began. Billy and Junior were gone, and Harvey was at the university, where he was rapidly becoming something of a celebrity. He had formed another musical group — a full-sized orchestra — and had given two violin recitals, both of which had been written up in the campus newspaper.

Lukie had thought Harvey's departure for Ann Arbor would leave a great void in her life, but it seemed she and Sally never had a minute to spare. Sally had been called back to the D & C. Lukie, in addition to her previous duties, now went down to the *Clarion* on Wednesday nights, when the paper was put to bed, to help with the folding and the stuffing. Once a week the girls rolled bandages at the Red Cross, and on weekends they helped out at the servicemen's canteen the Eastern Star had set up at the depot.

Ironically, Junior had ended up in the Navy; the induction center had had a quota to fill the day he reported. Sally shared his letters with Lukie in Homeroom. He had been assigned to the Navy's combat air-crewmen program, he had written. He would undergo training at Memphis and Miami, and then join a torpedo-bomber squadron at Fort Lauderdale. The new squadrons were being shipped out to the Pacific as soon as they were formed, but he was sure he would get a leave after he won his wings.

It seemed to Lukie there was no getting away from the war. In the fall, Higbie Manufacturing began making aerial flares for the Army. The flares were used to light targets in the night bombing raids the Allies were conducting over Europe. It disturbed Lukie that her town could be so intimately involved in the destruction of the great cities of Germany. She imagined some German Fräulein sifting through the rubble of her home and coming across one of the burned-out flares, with the Higbie imprint still showing. She would stare at it and wonder of the cruelty of Zebron Falls. She would know nothing of the tall elms that lined Wilcox Street, or of the way the mist came up off the river on an April morning, or of Billy Butts's great run in the homecoming game — only the single, terrible fact of the flare.

The production of the flares was very hazardous. They were made of a mixture of powdered magnesium and powdered aluminum, blended with various oxidizing agents. The blending was done by operators who worked

116

behind thick concrete shields, to protect them in the event of an explosion. Lukie worried that Uncle Farnie might be exposed to danger, but he continued to work in a separate part of the plant.

On Thanksgiving Day, Lukie decided that, one way or another, Uncle Farnie was going to share in the family's holiday meal. So after dinner she slipped out to the kitchen and fixed a plate to take to him. In the middle of it, her father walked in on her. She braced herself for a reprimand, but it never came.

"Take a wing," he instructed her. "Farnie always liked the wing best."

Lukie was speechless.

"And he likes gravy on his stuffing."

Sally went down to Uncle Farnie's place with Lukie that afternoon, for they were going to the second show at the Hills. They found Uncle Farnie great fun, and afterward they speculated on the identity of the woman with whom he had skated the twenty bridges.

"Mrs. LaBurge?" Sally joked.

"Ugh!" Lukie grimaced, and they both laughed.

"I know!" Sally lit up. "Miss Pray."

"Oh, Sally. That's ridiculous."

"It is not," Sally persisted. "She was just starting out as a librarian back then, and it had to be someone of her intellectuality. I mean, twenty bridges is — epic."

Ever since the week at Clam Lake, Sally had come increasingly under the influence of Miss Pray. She combed the library shelves for books on poetry and ballet and the Renaissance painters, and when Mitzelfeld's held its annual fall sale, she splurged and bought an outfit that frankly imitated one of Miss Pray's unorthodox ensembles — a tweed skirt and jacket, with brogues and a floppy hat.

"Well?" Sally said anxiously the day she tried it on for Lukie. "I think it looks rather British, don't you?"

Lukie doubled up, laughing.

But when Mr. Panella announced tryouts for the senior class play, *The Importance of Being Earnest,* it became dazzlingly evident that Sally's new interests were not merely a girlish flight of fancy. She easily won the role of Cecily, the ingénue, and Mr. Panella suggested she might want to study dramatics after graduation.

"It's amazing!" Lukie remarked to Lorena Pearsall. "And to think, in sixth grade she got stage fright playing one of the nymphs in the May Festival."

As seniors, Lukie and Sally enjoyed the prerogatives Zebron High traditionally accorded candidates for graduation. Freshmen idolized them, teachers flattered them, sophomores and juniors deferred to them. Mr. Severence began referring to them not as seniors but as the Class of '44 — thus confirming their identity in the long history of the school and of the community.

"It sounds so impressive," Sally said. "Like something you'd chisel in granite."

It was a time of purposeful activity. The class average was exceptionally high, and with a good showing on final exams there was a chance of setting a new school scholastic record. There was the yearbook to be written, scholarships to be applied for, branches of military service to be decided on —and beneath it all, the melancholy knowledge that soon a very special period of their lives would be ending.

And so Lukie Bishop's final year at Zebron High flew by in sweet anticipation of things to come — the senior prom, baccalaureate services, commencement, and, in the meantime, exciting weekends in Ann Arbor visiting Harvey. For the time being, at least, her world seemed in reasonably good order, save for one thing:

There was no word from Billy.

19

On the first Saturday in December, Lukie turned seventeen. As usual, she invited Uncle Farnie to her birthday party, and, as usual, he declined. But shortly after breakfast that morning, she received a call from Mr. Roscoe Martin, the lawyer. She was to come to Mr. Martin's office that afternoon, as soon as her Uncle Farnie got off work — and bring a dollar.

"What do you suppose he wants?" Lukie asked her mother, mystified.

"It's probably something to do with St. Philip's, dear. Isn't Mr. Martin on the vestry this year?"

"But what about Uncle Farnie?"

"Oh-h, perhaps he's become devout." Myrene Bishop smiled, a bit deceptively, Lukie thought. "It happens to men in middle age, you know."

The offices of Martin & Martin, Attorneys-at-Law,

were on the third floor of the Zebron Falls State Bank Building. Lukie climbed the stairway apprehensively, for the office of Dr. Barrett, the dentist, was on the same floor, and the antiseptic smells always filled her with dread.

She was ushered without delay into the musty old law office. Uncle Farnie was already there, still in his work clothes. Mr. Martin, a wrinkled, stoop-shouldered man, pushed some legal papers across the desk.

"Your uncle has a business matter to transact, Lukie," he explained. "If you'll kindly convey to him the sum of one dollar and then sign where I've indicated."

Lukie did as instructed. Then Mr. Martin handed her what appeared to be a deed and a bill of sale.

"Congratulations, young lady. You are now the owner of a forty-acre apple orchard."

Lukie turned to Uncle Farnie, astonished.

"It's your birthday present, sweetheart," he said. "I'm sorry I couldn't tie it in a ribbon."

"But Uncle Farnie!" Lukie protested, in tears. "It's your inheritance!"

"And now it's your inheritance, Lukie. Maybe you'll do better by it than I did." He gave her a little slap on the behind. "Now blow your nose and I'll treat you to a sarsaparilla over at the hotel."

The tap room was filled with after-work drinkers. Uncle Farnie's cronies waved to him from the bar. "Who's your girlfriend, Farnie?" they joked, and Lukie felt the sense of pride she always felt when she was with her uncle in public.

"I just can't get *over* it!" she exulted, scarcely able to

contain herself. "I own the orchard!" And then, soberly, "Oh, my gosh! What will I do with it?"

"Well, you could start working it," Uncle Farnie suggested, "and become the apple tycoon of Zebron Falls. Or you could sell it. The way land values have been soaring, it ought to bring a pretty fair price, with all that river frontage."

Uncle Farnie was in an expansive mood, and his health seemed better than it had in months. He set up drinks for the house and reminisced about the plan he'd had for the orchard when he was a boy — to build a mill down along the river and market his own cider.

"What a fine idea!" Lukie said brightly. "How come you never did it?"

"Oh, there was the war." Uncle Farnie shrugged. "And then things kept coming up. There's a timing to life. You've got to do a thing when the circumstances are right, or else it's no good."

"Is that why you never got married?" Lukie asked. "The timing?"

"You might say that." Uncle Farnie smiled.

"But it's not too late. I mean, you're not too old, and the girls at the mill think you're a regular Casanova. Besides, you're good with kids. You should have a dozen of your own."

Uncle Farnie laughed and shook his head.

"It wouldn't be any good. An uncle gets the fun of his nieces and nephews without the responsibility. No, if I had kids of my own I'd be crabbing at them as bad as your daddy."

122

"Nobody could crab that bad," Lukie said, making a face.

Uncle Farnie drained his stein of beer and signaled for another.

"Well, I'll tell you, Lukie," he said, "there are compensations for everything. If your daddy didn't crab at you the way he does, you wouldn't be half the person you are."

"I don't understand." Lukie frowned.

"I mean, it's toughened you up inside. Your daddy crabs at you, and you feel resentful, right? And so you keep trying to prove yourself and end up excelling in everything you do. Remember when you first started high school, how you were scared of your own shadow?"

Lukie felt uncomfortable at the turn in the conversation. She disliked talking about herself.

"And exactly how did you figure out all that?" she demanded.

"Oh, it was easy." Uncle Farnie winked. "That's how it was with me when I was your age. Your Grandpa Bishop used to berate me all over the place. Your daddy was always the steady one, and I was the black sheep. He was the halfback, I ran interference —"

"But you were always a team," Lukie put in, "weren't you?"

"Yes," Uncle Farnie allowed, "but he was always a notch above me. He was the pilot, I was the machine gunner. He was the lieutenant, I was the sergeant . . ."

The street lights were coming on as they got up to

123

leave. Crossing the hotel lobby, Uncle Farnie paused in front of an ornate wall mirror and tugged at the loose skin under his chin.

"It's funny how age creeps up on you," he said reflectively. "You keep shaving in front of the same mirror every day and don't notice it. Then you catch an unexpected glimpse of yourself and it's like a jolt — the lines, the bags, the wrinkles, staring at you like the awful truth."

He put an arm around Lukie, and the two of them walked out into the cold December evening.

"Did I ever tell you the wisdom of the ages, sweetheart," Uncle Farnie asked, "for all generations, all conditions, all situations?"

"No." Lukie giggled, expecting a joke.

"This, too, shall pass away."

Lukie watched Uncle Farnie walk down Main Street toward the bridge. He seemed a lonely figure, in his red mackinaw and with his lunch pail tucked under one arm.

"Thank you for the orchard, Uncle Farnie!" she called after him.

Uncle Farnie turned and waved, then continued on his way. Lukie hated seeing him go off by himself. She thought of him as a young man. He had skated twenty bridges up the river, clasping his girlfriend's mittened hand. How sweet it must have been! And then she thought of his narrow world now — from Higbie's to the tap room to his place behind Rosemergy's, with no one to comfort him when he woke in the night. It was as if his future had ended the day he got back from the war, and he wanted only to be left alone with the past.

How had it happened?

20

Wake up, dear." Myrene Bishop, in a faded house-coat and with her hair in curlers, gently shook Lukie's shoulder. "Harvey's on the phone."

Slowly, Lukie came awake.

"*Har*vey?" she said sleepily. "Good grief, what time is it, anyway?"

"Late." Her mother frowned. "It's a good thing your father didn't hear the phone."

Lukie slipped into her old wool robe and hurried down to the front hall.

"Harvey?" she said, picking up the phone. "What's wrong?"

"Wrong? Why should anything be wrong?"

"Oh honestly, Harvey, do you realize it's after midnight?"

"Oh," Harvey said lamely. "I hadn't noticed. I was

studying. Listen, I've got swell news. I've been invited to do the 'Scottish Fantasy' with the University Symphony Orchestra. Can you come over for the concert? It's sort of my debut. I've never performed with a full symphony before."

"When?"

"Saturday. There's a train that gets in at one. Don't be late. Hey, did I tell you about my dance orchestra? We're booked for the Military Ball . . ."

Myrene Bishop was in the kitchen fixing hot cocoa when Harvey finally hung up.

"I'm sorry he woke you, Mama." Lukie yawned. "He gets so wrapped up in his sharps and flats, he doesn't notice the time."

"He's a little self-centered, isn't he, dear?"

"Why do you say that?" Lukie asked defensively.

"Oh, he always seems to be putting his interests ahead of yours."

"It's just his temperament, Mama. A lot of artistic people are that way. Deep down, he's really very sensitive."

"Are you sure he's the right boy for you, Lukie? The two of you are opposites, you know."

"Oh, for Pete's sake, Mama!" Lukie said impatiently. "He's only a boyfriend. I mean, it's not as if we were going to elope, or something."

The excursion to Ann Arbor got off to a fine start, with a lovely ride on the North Star. Billy's Uncle Zeke, who was senior porter on the Michigan Central, spotted Lukie boarding the train at the depot and insisted that she sit in the observation lounge, where he made a special fuss over her. The crack train seemed to radiate an aura of

127

luxury and power as it sped through the rolling, snow-covered landscape. Uncle Zeke hadn't heard from Billy either, but he seemed unconcerned.

"Don't you worry about Billy." He smiled jovially as he served Lukie a complimentary ginger ale. "All the Jim Crow laws in the world aren't going to hold that boy down!"

In Detroit, it was necessary for Lukie to change to the Ann Arbor local, which was delayed while a troop train was cleared through. It was nearly one-thirty when the towers of the university came into view in the hills above the Huron River. Lukie liked Ann Arbor. She liked the turreted depot and the way the students sang the song about "old Ann Arbor town" when the trains pulled in. She liked the little campus shops and the beer places. There were bicycles everywhere, and at night the fraternity brothers serenaded their girls from under their windows.

"Holy cats!" Harvey said irritably as she clambered down from the train. "What took you so long, anyway?"

"There was a troop train . . ." Lukie started to explain.

"Never mind." Harvey grabbed her hand and waved for a taxi. "I'm going to be late."

"But what's the rush?" Lukie protested. "The concert isn't until tonight, is it?"

"Rehearsal, dummy," Harvey said, shaking his head in exasperation. "Did you think we make everything up as we go along?"

"The troop train wasn't my fault, Harvey." Lukie bristled — then caught herself. It was just his nerves, she

128

remembered, and starting a fight would only upset him more.

"Can you stay overnight?" he asked. "A girl in bassoons will put you up at the Pi Phi house."

"No," Lukie replied. "The Tuesday Musicale is singing at St. Philip's tomorrow. I've got to catch the last train back."

Harvey deposited her in front of the student union, then piled back into the cab.

"Have a Coke, or something," he called as the cab drove off. "I'll meet you here after rehearsal."

Lukie stood glumly at the curb, stranded. It was snowing. Lights were burning in the buildings of the great university, even though it was not yet three o'clock. Laughing couples hurried past her in the snow. For a minute, she had the feeling of being on the outside, looking in. With Harvey Toles, she was learning, nothing was ever the way you hoped it would be.

Harvey treated her to supper at a restaurant whose walls were lined with fraternity paddles. His disposition hadn't improved. He picked at his food and drummed on the table, and as they walked across the campus to the auditorium, he barely spoke two words. Lukie began to wonder why he had ever invited her in the first place.

Then, in the lobby of the auditorium, with the concertgoers beginning to arrive, he seemed to relax.

"You can go in and take your seat now," he said. "I've got to go backstage and change. Wait till you see my rented outfit — white tie and tails, yet."

He started across the lobby.

129

"Good luck, Harvey," Lukie called after him.

Suddenly, Harvey turned and came back.

"Thanks, Lukie," he said nervously, giving her a quick kiss and a hug.

Lukie breathed a deep sigh of relief. It was like seeing a sick person magically restored to health, and she knew that in some complex way Harvey needed her, really needed her.

"Thanks for what, silly?" She smiled pertly.

"For putting up with me. For everything."

"Will you be all right now, Harvey?"

"Yes, I'll be okay." He nodded, rubbing his eyes. "I've got to be okay."

Lukie had never attended a symphony concert before. The Shostakovich selection was loud and discordant, she thought. She found the Mendelssohn overture much more pleasing, and then Harvey came onstage and bowed stiffly. The conductor raised his baton, and as the opening bars of the "Scottish Fantasy" flooded out over the audience — Lukie forgave Harvey everything. It was as if she could smell the heather and see the Highlands, and certain solo passages were so unbearably sweet, she wept.

"I wanted it to last forever," she told Harvey as they were leaving the auditorium.

"I know." Harvey seemed pleased. "That's how I feel when I play it. But I haven't got the last movement right yet."

They walked up toward State Street, the main thoroughfare through the campus. The snow had stopped and the sky was clear. Harvey seemed a different person from a few hours ago, relaxed and confident.

"There's time for a snack before your train leaves," he said, squinting at his watch. "Is there any place special you'd like to go?"

"The place where they serve beer in pitchers and sing songs!" Lukie said eagerly. "My mother used to go there when she was a girl. Oh, I'm so glad you invited me!"

"I'm glad you came."

"Really and truly?" Lukie asked, taking Harvey's arm.

"Really and truly," Harvey said. "I don't know if I could've held together otherwise."

"Well, you're a basket case at times," Lukie teased him, "but you have your good points."

As they came to State Street, Lukie paused for a moment to look in a bookstore window. Harvey walked on a few paces ahead. When Lukie turned to catch up to him, she froze in terror. He was walking directly into the path of an oncoming car.

"Harvey!" she screamed.

But it was too late. Horns blared, brakes squealed, people shouted, and a pair of eyeglasses sailed through the air.

"Harvey!" Lukie cried, racing to his side. "Are you all right?"

Had it not been for the snow and the slippery streets, Harvey might have been killed. But as it was, traffic was moving slowly, and the impact of the collision merely hurled him into a soft bank of snow along the curb.

"I guess I wasn't looking," Harvey said sheepishly.

The driver of the car, an elderly professor, was quite shaken.

"There was nothing I could do!" he told the police

131

when they came. "The boy walked right in front of me!"

Lukie searched through the snow for Harvey's glasses, which were unbroken. Then the police officers drove the two of them to the university infirmary.

"I'm all right," Harvey kept insisting.

But the doctor at the infirmary had different ideas.

"Young man," he said firmly, "this university is responsible for your physical as well as your intellectual well-being. Twenty-four hours under observation isn't going to kill you. We'll take a few x-rays and run some tests."

Harvey turned to Lukie in embarrassment.

"Gee, Lukie," he apologized, "I'm sorry I ruined everything."

But Lukie wasn't thinking of the disrupted evening. All she could think of was one terrifying fact. Harvey had looked directly at the car that hit him but had not been able to see it.

21

On the day before Zebron High was to let out for Christmas vacation, Mr. Leiber summoned Lukie to his office.

"I understand you were with Harvey when he had the mishap in Ann Arbor," he said, waving her into a chair.

"Yes, sir," Lukie replied anxiously.

"Then I am sure you are aware that there are certain, ah, difficulties with his eyesight." Mr. Leiber seemed to be groping for the correct words. "There is no easy way of putting it. Harvey is going blind."

Lukie stared at him numbly.

"It is the result of an old injury. When he was fifteen, there was an accident . . ."

"At the swimming pond?" Even as Lukie asked, she sensed the answer.

"Yes." Mr. Leiber nodded. "There was some scuffling

on the footbridge, and Harvey got knocked over the dam. You were there that day?"

"Yes, sir," Lukie answered weakly. "I was there."

"The damage appeared to have healed, but glaucoma is an insidious disease — no pain, no warning until it is too late . . ."

Lukie gazed out the window. It was a gray, overcast day. Beyond the snow-covered rooftops, she could see the North Star rushing down the valley, its horn blaring and its gold markings crusted with ice from the frozen forests of Michigan's north country. One summer afternoon, she thought, she and Billy had ridden the North Star up to Tienken Junction, and now Harvey was going blind because of that trip.

"Harvey's father and I have been aware of the prognosis for some time," Mr. Leiber was saying. "We had hoped his vision would hold up at least until he finished at the university, but apparently the deterioration has been more rapid than the doctors anticipated."

"Does Harvey know?" Lukie asked.

"He didn't — until he walked in front of that car. The doctors at the student infirmary discovered the condition and told him. He will need all the support we can give him. I was over to see him yesterday. He seemed in a daze."

"But what about his music, Mr. Leiber? His career?"

Mr. Leiber fiddled with a tuft of white hair that grew from his ear. "In one sense, it needn't be affected at all," he said. "Some of our greatest performing artists are sightless. But there will be certain practical difficulties."

Harvey had two choices, he explained. He could stay

at the university long enough to get a teaching certificate and then seek a position in education — at Zebron High, perhaps. The school would be expanding soon, and there would be many changes. It would be a good life for him, a secure life, and he would be among friends. But even that would require major resources. Soon he would need a companion, someone to read his textbooks to him and to keep him from walking in front of cars. Also, instruction in braille should be commenced. It would be costly, even at a state university, and Harvey's father had little money.

"And the other choice?" Lukie asked.

"Scholarships for the blind are available at certain eastern conservatories," Mr. Leiber replied. "The competition is very keen, but I believe Harvey would have a chance."

All of his needs would be met, he said. It would be a new kind of life for him, an intense life, a life devoted solely to his music. And if he were to succeed — then he would belong to the world of conductors and virtuosos and great concert orchestras.

"It is a very special world," he said, "a very possessive world, and there might not be room in it for anything else — not even a wife or a lover."

The bell rang. Lukie started to collect her books.

"If it were you, Mr. Leiber," she asked earnestly, "which would you choose?"

Mr. Leiber threw up his hands and sighed.

"Frankly, I am glad the choice is not mine to make. Either course would offer important rewards. My years at Zebron High have been the most contented of my career. I look upon the small towns of America as one of the great achievements of civilization. For Harvey to share his artistic vision with the young people of the community — this could be deeply satisfying. It will depend on Harvey, on what he values most in life — on what he loves most."

He got to his feet and came around the desk.

"The next few weeks will be critical," he said. "He must accept his failing eyesight not as a handicap but simply as an obstacle that can be overcome."

Lukie made an excuse to Sally that afternoon and walked home alone — by way of the village park, which ran along both sides of the creek that had been dammed to form a swimming pond. The park seemed bleak and desolate in the gray December afternoon. A wooden footbridge, which also served as a diving platform, ran above the dam. Lukie walked out onto the bridge and looked down at the foaming waters. She remembered it all as if it were yesterday — the commotion on the bridge, the shrill screeching of the lifeguard's whistle, the boy in blue swimming trunks washed up on the sharp rocks below the dam.

It had begun innocently enough — with a bet with Junior over who would be the first to ride the North Star, which had inaugurated service to Zebron Falls that day. Uncle Zeke had let her and Billy ride the four miles up to the Junction. They had walked back to town along the tracks, and as they were cutting through the park, Junior had come up behind Lukie and shoved her into the pond with her clothes on. Lukie was furious. She splashed out of the pond and chased Junior up on the crowded footbridge. Billy was the only person who saw the entire chain reaction of mishaps that followed. "You'd better scram, ol' buddy," he had told her. "You knocked that kid into the dam." She remembered leaving the park and hurrying up Wilcox Street. The heat of the sidewalk burned her bare feet, and her wet dress left a trickle of water behind her. Going by Bebout's, she had caught a glimpse of herself in the window — the dirty face, the matted hair, the wet dress clinging to her legs. She was a misfit, she had thought, an ugly duckling, and when she started high school everybody would laugh at her . . .

The whistle at the knitting mill roused her from her reverie. She crossed the bridge and hurried through the park. It was growing dark. Christmas lights shone from the houses. She wondered what it would be like to be blind. Walking up Ludlow Street, she shut her eyes for two blocks. She felt dizzy, and kept losing her balance. Twice she stumbled into snowdrifts, and crossing Fifth Street she tripped on the curb and skinned her knee.

Tears came to her eyes. She would make it up to him, she promised herself. Somehow.

22

Harvey came home for Christmas vacation two days later. Lukie went down to the depot to meet him. It was snowing again. The snow made swirling patterns in the headlight of the locomotive as the train came to a stop.

The train was crowded with young men in uniform. Harvey was the last one off. Lukie bit her lip when she saw him. He looked tired and pale, and his eyes were puffy as if from lack of sleep. Stepping down to the platform, he tripped over one of his bags, and Lukie nearly burst into tears.

"Easy does it, son." The conductor caught Harvey by the arm.

They stood on the platform for a minute after the train had pulled out, neither of them knowing what to say. Finally, Harvey smiled uneasily.

"You know?" he asked.

"Yes," Lukie replied. "Mr. Leiber told me."

"Does it change anything?"

"Of course not, silly," Lukie answered softly. "Why would it change anything?"

She picked up one of Harvey's bags and took his hand.

"Come on," she said. "Let's drop off your things and then take a nice long walk."

They walked in the night in the snow, across the bridge and up South Hill, then back down Main Street to the Sweet Shoppe. Since her talk with Mr. Leiber, Lukie had inquired at Hartwig Real Estate about the market value of the orchard. It would bring a substantial amount, more than enough to meet Harvey's special requirements at the university over the next three years. But when she told Harvey her plan, she immediately regretted it.

"No!" he said sharply, a flash of anger in his eyes. "A guy can't take money from a girl."

Lukie dipped a French fry in catsup and stuffed it in his mouth.

"But when you're married," she said, smiling, "it's supposed to be share and share alike."

"You mean . . ."

"Of course, silly. We could rent a basement apartment near the campus. I'd be your guide, and do your reading, and help you with your braille lessons; and if we needed extra money I could take a part-time job at one of the bookstores, or something."

She waited for Harvey to respond. He stirred the ice in his Coke thoughtfully.

"Did you know that Beethoven was deaf?" he asked.

Lukie felt rebuffed. Perhaps it was too soon, she thought. Perhaps it made him feel too — dependent.

"I guess for a musician," she said, "being deaf would be worse than being blind."

"Yes," Harvey said, brightening. "I suppose it would. Of course, when you're blind you have to memorize everything. I mean, you couldn't very well stand up there and say, 'Excuse me a minute, folks, while I feel my music.' "

But later, as they were walking home through the cemetery, Harvey fell to brooding about the many things he wouldn't be able to do when his eyes finally gave out. Impulsively, Lukie pulled him into the shadows under the statue of Joshua Zebron and kissed him lightly on the lips.

"You don't need eyes to do that, Harvey," she whispered.

They stood under the statue in a quiet embrace. Lukie could feel a growing urgency in Harvey. His hand moved inside her coat and pressed insistently against her blouse. Her heart pounded. Maybe if she let him go ahead he wouldn't feel so depressed. She thought of the loft and felt a fluttering sensation in her stomach. There were pillows and thick quilts that kept you warm even on cold winter nights. Harvey's fingers were fumbling with her buttons now, and his other hand was doing something with her skirt. It would be so easy, she thought, and they wouldn't have to do *everything*. And then the lights of a passing car flashed through the cemetery. Lukie used the intrusion as an excuse to slip away.

"Come on," she said, kissing Harvey on the cheek and

taking his hand. "I'll make popcorn and we'll sit in the sunroom."

And for the rest of the evening she reproached herself for not being able to finish what she had started. Nearly all the girls went part of the way. She had cheated Harvey. With his world collapsing around him, the least she could have done was — that.

23

It turned out to be a hopeful holiday season. The news from the war fronts was good. The Navy had won several important victories in the Pacific. The Russians had broken out of Stalingrad, and the American Army in Italy was pushing toward Cassino. There was talk that the Allies would soon launch an invasion from England and begin a great drive into Germany. Lukie began to hope the war might be over before graduation.

One morning, Myrene Bishop came up from the mailbox, waving a letter.

"It's from Billy, dear!" she called.

Lukie raced up to her room and tore open the envelope. It was a funny Christmas card, from an Army Air Corps base in Texas, with a note jotted on the back. Billy said very little about his new duties, but Lukie could tell he was in good spirits, and if he was still a waiter, he seemed to be accepting the fact philosophically.

The next day, Sally received a letter and a snapshot from Junior, who was now undergoing aerial-gunnery training in Miami.

"Doesn't he look lean and tan!" She glowed as she handed the picture to Lukie.

It had been taken on a firing range, with Junior in dungarees and a white sailor's hat. An ammunition belt was slung over his shoulder. Sally let Lukie read the letter. He had gone swimming in the ocean several times, Junior had written, but it didn't seem right to be lolling on the beach in the middle of December, and he missed the snow. When Lukie got down to the last paragraph, Sally snatched the letter away.

"Words between lovers," she trilled airily, "should be written on the wind."

"Sally, you're not!" Lukie gasped.

"Not what?"

"Lovers."

Sally smiled mysteriously. "Wouldn't you like to know," she teased, with a toss of her head.

"But when could you have?" Lukie demanded. "*Where* could you have?"

"Well . . ." Sally admitted, "that's about the only thing that's stopped us. I mean, cars are so cramped, and can you imagine the picnic Mrs. LaBurge would have if she spotted Junior sneaking me into the Saint James Hotel?"

"Without luggage, yet," Lukie commented with a giggle.

But deep down she worried that Sally might get herself in trouble. Junior would probably be coming home on leave before summer. She knew there were things the boys bought at Crissman's Drugs, but they seemed so mechanical, and she'd heard you couldn't trust them. She had seen one once, trampled in the litter along the path up on Squirrel Road, like a shriveled-up balloon. And staring at it and knowing what it had been used for, an odd excitement had come over her. Ever since, there had been nights when she felt an indefinable urgency deep in her somewhere, and on those nights she would squeeze her thighs and toss restlessly and dream of a shadowy, faceless boy who came into her room and did things with her. She was never able to identify the boy, but she knew it wasn't Harvey; he didn't have Harvey's nervous gestures.

As Christmas approached, Harvey seemed to be adjusting to his new circumstances more rapidly than any of them had hoped. He and Lukie saw each other every day. They went tobogganing and skating, and spent two days building an igloo on the high school lawn, as part of the town's annual snow sculpture competition.

"It's not as if I'd been born blind," Harvey said one day. "I mean, I've seen nineteen winters — and springs and summers and autumns. I guess I ought to remember what they look like."

"I'll be your eyes, Harvey," Lukie said. "I'll be your seeing-eye girl."

But an incident occurred that she was unable to put out of her mind. When the igloo was finished, Harvey started to crawl through the little tunnel-like entrance. It turned out that they had made the opening too narrow, and his shoulders got wedged.

"I'm stuck!" he cried. "Quick, help me!"

Lukie grabbed his ankles and pulled him free, thinking he'd somehow gotten hurt. But it wasn't that at all.

"I can't stand cramped places." He shivered, and a comparison flashed through Lukie's mind — Billy wouldn't have panicked.

"When you're thrown from a horse," she reminded him, "you're supposed to climb right back on. Remember?"

"But it's just an igloo," he replied, and he refused to try again, even after Lukie had packed down the snow to enlarge the opening.

"My hands are getting stiff," he said, discouraged. "I'd better soak them in warm water."

Two nights before Christmas, the full Tuesday Musicale, as was its tradition, went caroling through the streets of the town, with bells and candles and Mr. Panella dressed up as Santa Claus. The singers assembled in front of the St. James Hotel.

"Everybody meet back at the hotel afterward!" Miss Pray instructed, clapping her hands. "There'll be a little surprise!"

There was a fine holiday spirit in the air. The houses were lit up with colorful Yule displays. People waved from the windows and came out on the porches.

"Merry Christmas!" they called to the carolers.

To everybody's amazement, Miss Pray's surprise turned

out to be a party announcing her engagement to Mr. Panella.

"Miss Pray!" Lukie and Sally squealed. "How wonderful!"

The reception room off the hotel lobby was strung with holly and mistletoe. There was a buffet of ham and turkey and spiced pears, as well as a sparkling champagne punch with chunks of fruit floating in it.

"I just can't believe it!" Lukie exclaimed, and she wished Billy were there to witness the outcome of his matchmaking.

Miss Pray looked girlish and demure. The wedding would be held the last week in June, she said — at St. Andrew's, with a reception afterward in the church basement. They would honeymoon up at Mackinac Island, at the Grand Hotel.

"But I don't imagine we'll spend much time sitting on the veranda." She laughed — and Mr. Panella, still in his Santa Claus suit, nearly choked on a spiced pear.

Mr. Seed came by with his big Speed Graphic camera to take pictures for the *Clarion*.

"Ho, ho, ho!" he ribbed Mr. Panella. "Does Mrs. Claus know you've been stepping out on her?"

Miss Pray let the girls each have a little cup of punch.

"It tickles!" Sally giggled, her eyes watering and her cheeks flushing.

It was nearly midnight when the party broke up. Harvey wanted to walk Lukie home, but she didn't want him stumbling around in the dark by himself. Instead, the girls escorted Harvey down to the news agency. The punch had made Sally very giddy.

146

"On the first day of Christmas," she crooned as they crossed Main Street, "my true love gave to me-e . . ."

"Oh, honestly, Sally." Lukie laughed, yanking her up on the sidewalk. "I think I liked you better when you were an unknown."

At the news agency, the girls waved good night to Harvey, then started home. It was snowing again, thick, wet flakes that clung to the trees and gave a muffled quality to the sounds of the night.

"Oh, Lukie, I feel so happy!" Sally breathed deeply of the cold night air. "It's as if everything in life is starting to open up to us."

She talked animatedly about Junior and their plans for the future. After the war they were going to be married and live at his parents' place up in Harbor Springs. She was going to work as a waitress while Junior tried to write.

"But what will you do in the meantime?" Lukie asked.

"I don't know," Sally said. "I might go live with my aunt in Chicago till Junior gets discharged. Miss Pray says there's a ballet company in Chicago, and a theater group, and that they both accept amateurs. Wouldn't it be wonderful if I became an actress and Junior wrote me a play, or something?"

They walked past Pocock's Market and across Walnut Street. As they went by St. Andrew's, Lukie impulsively grabbed Sally's hand and turned in to the church.

"Come on," she said. "I want to light a candle for Billy."

"At this hour?" Sally said doubtfully.

"It's all right," Lukie assured her. "Catholic churches never close. You can light one for Junior, if you like."

"But Junior's a Presbyterian."

"What difference does that make, silly?"

Inside, the church was dark except for the flickering light of the vigil candles. A steam radiator hissed in the vestibule.

"Billy used to take me to mass with him when we were kids," Lukie said. "It's like Saint Philip's, only with Latin."

They stamped the snow from their boots, then tiptoed up the aisle to a rack of candles in front of one of the side altars. A Nativity scene was arranged around the altar — a manger, with statues of Mary and Joseph and the Baby Jesus. Lukie pulled off her mittens and fished two dimes from her coat pocket. The girls took turns lighting candles, then Lukie dropped the dimes in the coin box.

"You're supposed to say a prayer," she whispered. "Let's do it out loud. Nobody'll hear us."

"What should we say?" Sally asked, her blue eyes shining in the candlelight.

"We could wish them a merry Christmas."

"All right."

They slipped into a pew and knelt with their heads bowed. Their simple prayer echoed through the darkened church.

"Merry Christmas, Billy."

And then: "Merry Christmas, Junior."

And then, unaccountably, Lukie felt her eyes filling with tears. She looked over at Sally and saw that she was crying, too.

"Oh, Lukie, do you think they're all right?"

After a while, they wiped their eyes and put on their mittens and went out into the snow-filled night.

24

Winter broke in late February that year. By the middle of March, the ice and snow had melted away, and the smells of spring were in the air.

Word had come a month ago that Billy had been transferred again — this time to Chanute Field, an air base in Illinois. One day, Lukie walked over to see Billy's mother and father. Ella Butts was just taking a banana cake from the oven. She served Lukie a piece still warm, with a glass of milk, and Henry Butts showed her a snapshot Billy had sent them. Billy was posed jauntily against the propeller of an airplane, and his uniform seemed somehow different.

"It's like pulling teeth to get any information out of that boy," Mr. Butts complained. "Either he's the best potato peeler in the Army Air Corps, or . . ."

"Or what, Mr. Butts?" Lukie asked.

"Or he's got something up his sleeve."

When she got home, Mr. Toles phoned. He was going over to Ann Arbor for Dads' Day on Saturday, he said, and suggested Lukie make the trip with him.

"I'd love to, Mr. Toles," Lukie said. "I'll meet you at the depot."

But deep down she felt resentful. She had planned to set out her onion plants this weekend; the soil was just right, wet but not mucky, and next week it might be too dry. And she resented Mr. Toles's assumption in extending the invitation. She knew she had encouraged this attitude, but her life seemed to be overflowing with obligations, and she was beginning to feel hemmed in.

However, on the morning she and Mr. Toles were to leave for Ann Arbor, Lukie noticed some disturbing stains on Lady's mat next to the bed. She bent down for a closer look. It appeared to be pus mixed with blood, and there was a sickly sweetish odor. She hurried downstairs.

"Where's Lady, Mama?"

"I saw her loping down toward the orchard a while ago, dear."

"Mama, please call Mr. Toles and tell him I can't go. Something's wrong with Lady. I've got to take her over to Dr. Bortman's."

It was a disease called pyometra, Dr. Bortman said, a massive infection of the uterus. The condition required immediate surgery, but Lady's heart was too weak to withstand an operation. There was no hope. The discharge would get worse, then become a torrent as the infection spread to other organs.

151

"She will be very thirsty. All you can do is keep her as comfortable as possible and see that she has plenty of fresh water."

"How long?" Lukie asked.

"A few days; a few weeks. There's no telling."

He put a sympathetic arm around Lukie. He was a small, dark-haired man who always became personally involved with the animals he treated.

"There will be pain," he said. "If it's severe, call me and I'll . . . well, we don't want Lady to suffer, do we?"

Four days later, when Lukie came home from school, Lady had gone off to die. She found the dog in her place above the river — lying on her side in a soft patch of grass, her breath coming in shallow whimpers and her head facing the river, as if she wanted one final look at it.

"Good girl, Lady," Lukie whispered, stroking the great German shepherd's muzzle. "Good girl."

She stayed with the dog till dusk. Then when the whimpers became moans, she went back to the house, her eyes brimming with tears, and called Dr. Bortman.

"Can you come right away? The pain is very bad. I'll meet you in the orchard."

Lukie kept stroking Lady's muzzle till the end. It was over quickly. Lady made a little whoosh, like a sigh of relief that she'd finally come to rest — and was gone.

"It's always difficult," Dr. Bortman said. "I see it every day, and yet I've never gotten used to it. You feel the life go out of them and wonder where they've gone."

He had brought the puppy he had once promised, he said — a fine mixed shepherd, four months old, with a silver gray coat and a blue cast to her eyes. She had belonged to a couple up on Snell Road who had moved away when the husband was drafted.

"Her name is Schatzie. She's up in the truck. Would you like to get acquainted?"

"No, sir, not right now. Would you take her up to the house and tell Buddy to look after her?"

"Lady was an old dog, Lukie," Dr. Bortman said, "and she had a good life. You can't let it tear at you."

But all Lukie could think of was that Lady was gone.

"We grew up together," she said tightly. "We went everywhere together. I washed her in catsup when she tangled with skunks."

She buried Lady in the orchard. Buddy wanted to help with the digging, but Lukie chased him away; and when she brought Lady's body down from the bluffs in a wheelbarrow, she wouldn't let anyone help. It was dark when she slipped up the back stairway to her room. The new puppy, she discovered, had taken over the mat next to the bed.

"Get out of Lady's bed," Lukie screamed, "you stupid little dog!"

And then she threw herself on the bed and cried herself to sleep.

In the morning, Buddy rapped on the door. Lukie was at her desk next to the dormer, writing a letter.

"Lukie . . ." Buddy said bashfully.

"Yes, Buddy?"

"Can Schatzie be my dog? I mean, Lady was always your dog, and — well, all the other guys have dogs that follow them to school and wait for them at the matinee on Saturdays."

"Yes, Buddy." Lukie smiled, tousling her brother's hair. "Schatzie can be your dog."

And then she took a piece of paper and drew a little map on it.

"This is the way to my secret hiding place," she said, handing the map to Buddy. "It's yours now."

"For keeps?" Buddy said, wide-eyed.

"For keeps. I don't need it anymore."

When Buddy had gone, Lukie returned to her letter. She read what she had written, then tore it up and started again.

April 8, 1944

Dear Billy,
   If it is at all possible, please come home . . .

25

With Lady's death, Lukie came to the realization that she could never sell the orchard, that indeed she had never really intended to. The orchard was hallowed ground now, and selling it would be a desecration. But beyond that, she felt a need to keep intact the last remnant of the old family farm, perhaps even to restore some measure of the vitality the place had known before hard times — as Uncle Farnie might have done if life had turned out differently for him.

She did not tell Harvey any of this. Since Christmas, he had made no mention of the future of their relationship, nor had she. With graduation not far off, there had been a subtle change in her thinking, a kind of ordering of priorities. High school, she was discovering, offered a certain safety. Things could be put off; plans could be altered. You could decide to be a teacher one day, then switch to nursing the next. Romances blossomed and faded, with nobody the worse for it. There was margin for error and misjudgment, and you could test your wings.

But her situation with Harvey was different. From the start, she had envisioned their relationship in terms of the love stories she'd seen in movies — tender stories of guilt and atonement, in which the heroine sacrificed her life to the fulfillment of some great creative artist who had been handicapped through her carelessness. The trouble was, at the show the lights always came on when the movie was over, but with Harvey everything was for keeps — and she wondered if she might be dramatizing her sense of obligation toward him to a point of no return.

And so she proceeded with the orchard as if their conversation at the Sweet Shoppe had never happened. She marked Lady's grave with a large rock, then consulted her nursery catalogs for an apple tree — a Duchess would be appropriate, she decided — to plant over the grave when the soil warmed. Poring over nursery and seed catalogs always filled her with a pleasant sense of anticipation. She wanted to order every item listed, to experiment and take risks; and as the days went by a new plan for the orchard began to take shape in her mind. She remembered Uncle Farnie's boyhood dream of a cider mill along the river. A mill, yes, and more modern than Mr. Yates's — but why sell only cider? There could be a store — a special kind of store that sold only homemade or home-grown produce — fruits and vegetables, jams and cheeses, pies and cakes. There was no end to the possibilities — pottery, needlepoint, even turkeys in season. The trick would be to establish dependable resources, farmers and housewives, who could keep you supplied on a regular basis. And, eventually, why not a full-scale fruit farm? You could do a lot with forty acres — apples and pears, peaches and plums, grapes and berries.

The idea received support from an unexpected source — her father.

"It sounds realistic," he agreed. "And you've got a good head for business."

It was a misty April evening, the first day of Easter vacation, and Lukie had run into him in the orchard.

"Of course, you'd be handicapped by lack of expertise," he went on. "Any kind of farming is highly scientific these days. But I suppose you could read books and pick up a few pointers from Henry Butts."

They walked down toward the river. The fields looked brown and sodden, but the apple buds were beginning to swell and blossom, and there were touches of color from the first flowers of spring — violets and shad blossoms and waxen white bloodroots.

"It was a fine thing for your Uncle Farnie to do," Walter Bishop said; "signing the orchard over to you. Years back, I wanted him to sell it, but I'm glad now that he didn't."

"Was that when we had to sell off the rest of the land?" Lukie asked.

"Yes," her father replied. "We would have gotten a better price if the orchard had been included."

He pointed to a tree with a particularly gnarled trunk. It was the largest tree in the orchard.

"That's a Cox Orange Pippin," he said. "It was always Farnie's favorite tree. There isn't a finer dessert apple in the world."

At the river's edge, they stood in silence for a while, looking down at the swiftly moving stream.

"It will be a backbreaking job, you know," Walter Bishop said. "The orchard has been neglected since the early years of the Depression."

"Yes, sir, I know."

"And what about college? I won't force it on you, but there'll be enough money to see you through four years — not luxuriously, but comfortably."

"I don't know, Daddy. I'm really not sure about anything yet."

"Well, let me know if you need any help with the orchard. I'll be getting an assistant at the mill in a few weeks, and there'll be more time for me to be with you and Beth and Buddy."

"How wonderful!"

"Yes." Walter Bishop gave an embarrassed smile. "You've practically grown up while my back was turned. We'll have to get acquainted all over again."

He started up to the house, then turned back.

"By the way," he said, "graduation isn't too far off. Are you planning to have an open-house after the commencement ceremony?"

"If it's all right with you," Lukie replied.

"Of course," her father said — and paused. "Why don't you invite your Uncle Farnie?"

Lukie held her breath. A reunion was within reach, she sensed, and she didn't want to ruin it by saying the wrong thing.

"May I tell him you said so, Daddy? Otherwise he won't come."

Her father said nothing.

"May I, Daddy?"

"All right," he finally said. He was trying to appear nonchalant, Lukie knew, but his speech impediment from the war flared up and gave him away. "You c-c-can tell Farnie that, if you l-l-like."

The following afternoon, Lukie went over to Sally's house to work on the class prophecy. It was nearly supper time when she got home. As she hung her coat in the front hall closet, something in the parlor caught her attention. It was her portrait, the one that had been gathering dust in the attic for so many years, hanging above the mantel.

"How come you decided to put my portrait back up?" she asked her mother in the kitchen.

"I didn't, dear," Myrene Bishop answered from the stove, where she was ladling beef stew into a thermos jar. "It was your father's idea."

Lukie sank into a chair and felt a warm glow come over her. He is coming to terms with me, she thought, and she smiled. Or were they coming to terms with each other?

"Who's the thermos for?" she asked her mother.

"Your father has to work late tonight."

"I'll take it down to him."

"Oh, you needn't bother, Lukie."

"It's no bother, Mama. And I'll get up early and fix his breakfast while school's out. I mean, mothers need a vacation once in a while, too, don't you think?"

"If you insist, dear."

And Myrene Bishop turned to the sink to conceal her smile.

26

The explosion rocked Zebron Falls three days after Easter vacation. Lukie had just come into her fifth-hour calculus class. She hurried to the windows. To the east, a cloud of black smoke hovered over Higbie Manufacturing. Sirens began to wail. People were hurrying out into the streets. A fire truck raced up Water Street. Lukie felt her heart pounding. For an instant she thought this must be what an air raid was like. Then a second blast shook the town, and she could see orange flames shooting up into the rain-filled sky. She let her books clatter to the floor.

"Uncle Farnie!" she screamed, and ran from the room.

Higbie Manufacturing resembled the disaster scenes Lukie had seen in the newsreels. Ambulances were arriving by the time she raced up Water Street — coatless, her blouse hanging out from her gray flannel skirt, and her hair wet from the rain. State Police troopers were roping off the area to hold back the crowd. A searing, acrid odor filled the air. They had been blending chemicals for the aerial flares, she heard someone say, and something had gone wrong. The first explosion had demolished the new addition that had been built last summer; the second blast had torn into the main part of the plant.

"Stay back, please!" one of the troopers shouted.

Lukie slipped under the rope when the trooper's back was turned. She looked about frantically for Uncle Farnie. The fire appeared to be under control, but victims were still being led from the ruins, dazed and bloody. She stumbled over a body that had been dragged out into the street and hastily covered with a blanket. The blanket had become blood-soaked. Dear God, she prayed as she knelt beside the lifeless form, don't let it be Uncle Farnie! She pulled back the blanket and nearly fainted. The man's head had been crushed, and one of his arms was missing — but it wasn't Uncle Farnie.

And then she heard a familiar bellowing voice.

"By God, this town needs a hospital, and I'm going to see that it gets one!"

It was Mr. Seed, hurrying about with his Speed Graphic camera. Lukie rushed up to him.

"Have you seen Uncle Farnie, Mr. Seed?"

"They just took him to the hospital, Lukie — Saint Joe's, over in Pontiac."

Lukie turned and started to run off, but Mr. Seed grabbed her by the shoulder.

"It doesn't look good for him, Lukie. He got caught in the second blast. I think his lungs got scorched."

Lukie hitched a ride to Pontiac in a passing creamery truck. The driver took her directly to the main entrance of the big red brick hospital.

"You're soaked," he said. "You should have a coat on."

"I'll be all right," Lukie answered vaguely. "I'm very strong."

The hospital was a scene of great confusion. Ambulances were pulling in and out of the emergency entrance. The lobby was filling up with friends and relatives of the blast victims. Lukie pushed through the crowd to the information desk. Uncle Farnie was on the third floor, the nun told her. She could take the elevator.

"Thank you, Sister," Lukie mumbled.

The third floor was as hectic as the lobby. Beds had been set up in the corridors to accommodate the overflow of patients. Doctors worked on the victims where they found them. Nuns in long white robes hurried about with bandages and hypodermics and jars of blood with little rubber hoses attached to them. Lukie approached one of the nuns.

"Please, Sister, my uncle . . ."

The nun went to a desk and consulted a chart.

"Dr. Geist is with him," she said. "He is a very sick man. He requires an oxygen tent, but all of ours are in use. We have sent to Royal Oak." She threw up her hands in despair. "There were so many casualties, we simply were not equipped . . ."

Lukie went to the visitors' lounge to wait. She huddled in a chair in the corner and stared numbly out the window. It was growing dark. Neon lights were coming on in the business district. The city looked dismal in the

163

rain. Smoke billowed up from the factories, and water sprayed from the wheels of passing cars. So this was how it ended for Uncle Farnie, she thought. He should be in his old bed, in the house where he was born, looking out at his beloved orchard and with the family gathered around him.

After a while, Lukie noticed Mrs. LaBurge out in the corridor with two of her Eastern Star friends. Then Mr. Seed hurried into the lounge.

"It's Wednesday, you know," he said. "If you don't feel up to coming in tonight, don't worry about it, but sometimes work takes your mind off things."

"Yes," Lukie said. "I'll try to be there."

"The paper will be late. It will take time to set up the story on the explosion and get the cuts back from the engraver's. How is your Uncle Farnie?"

"They've sent for an oxygen tent."

"Well . . ." Mr. Seed took a deep breath. "Hope for the best. I talked to your mother. She's on her way over."

"And my father?" Lukie asked anxiously.

"Yes, he's coming, too."

Several minutes passed. Then Lukie felt a hand on her shoulder. It was the nun again.

"Miss Bishop?"

"Yes, Sister?"

"You must prepare yourself. He is failing rapidly."

"But the oxygen tent . . ."

"The damage is too great. His lungs have lost the capacity to get sufficient oxygen into the bloodstream."

"May I see him?"

"This way," the nun said, taking Lu' ie's hand. "He has been sedated."

And then it all became a blur. Uncle Farnie seemed in a stupor, as if he were hearing her from a distance. "I'm going to work the orchard, Uncle Farnie, just the way you said, and I'll carve your initials in the big Cox Orange Pippin." Oh, why didn't he answer! And then her mother was there, with Beth and Buddy in tow. Uncle Farnie seemed to rally briefly, as if he had been hoarding one last flicker of life for — for — why, of course, for the girl with the mittened hand! "Twenty bridges, Reenie," he whispered to Myrene Bishop. "Even the kids can't top it."

"Save your strength, Farnie, Walter's coming. Can you hear me, Farnie? Walter's coming."

And then Lukie's father was in the room, gaunt and uncertain. The rest of them stood back as he approached the bed — slowly, tentatively. "Hello, Farnie, how's the b-b-boy?"

"Hello, Walter, long time no see."

And at long last, the Buttermilk Twins were reunited.

Myrene Bishop herded the children out into the hall and closed the door behind her. Mr. Seed came over and waited with them. Half an hour passed. Then the door opened and Walter Bishop came out of the room.

"He's gone," he said vacantly. "He just drifted away on me . . ."

And then he slumped into a chair and buried his face in his hands and wept.

"Mrs. Bishop," the nun said softly. "If you please, there are some papers that must be filled out."

165

"Yes, of course," Myrene Bishop replied. "Children, your father and I will be a few minutes."

"I'll take them down to the car, Reenie," Mr. Seed volunteered. "You and Walter take all the time you need."

Lukie and Beth and Buddy followed Mr. Seed down the hall to the elevator. Beth had brought along Lukie's slicker.

"Sally brought it over. She said you'd left it at school."

Lukie's clothes were damp and wrinkled, and her face was smudged from the smoke of the fire. She tucked in her blouse and tried to smooth out her skirt. She wondered why she wasn't crying. She supposed the tears would come later.

"Who's going to take care of the funeral, Lukie?" Buddy asked.

"We are, Buddy. We're his family."

Down on the main floor, the crowd had thinned out a bit. Lukie noticed Beatrice LaBurge and the Eastern Star ladies sitting on a couch, gossiping. She could hear Mrs. LaBurge whispering.

"Well, why shouldn't he give her the orchard? She's his love child, isn't she?"

Lukie felt a sinking sensation go through her. Quickly, she looked around to see who had heard. Beth and Buddy were already past the information desk, but Mr. Seed, she was sure, had heard every word.

"Lukie," Buddy asked, "can I sleep in your room tonight?"

"Yes, Buddy."

And then she hurried out of the hospital and into the black, rainy night.

27

Beatrice LaBurge lived alone in a brick bungalow on Harrison Street, a block from the high school. Lukie waited in the shelter of a catalpa tree. It was still raining. The rain beat on her yellow slicker and trickled off the brim of her matching oilskin hat. A train whistle wailed in the night. She would stop at Potere's on the way home from the *Clarion*, she decided. Mr. Potere had said the body wouldn't be laid out till morning, but she didn't want to leave Uncle Farnie alone at the funeral home.

And so the dark family secret was out. Or was it? Mr. Seed had warned her you couldn't believe half of what Mrs. LaBurge said, that she manufactured gossip faster than a duck did fat, that he would have fired her years ago, but all she had in the world was her cat and her column and an annuity from the husband she'd hounded to the grave before he was forty.

167

Still — it all seemed to fit. It explained her father's crabbing and the falling-out with Uncle Farnie. It explained Uncle Farnie's special fondness for her and his giving her the orchard.

And if it was true, did it matter? Yes — at least the wild-oats part of it. She believed in standards and orderly relationships. There should be a propriety to things, and to have your conception be the result of a casual indiscretion was shabby and unacceptable.

And the other part, the possibility that all along Uncle Farnie might have been her father — did that matter? She didn't know. It shouldn't, instinct and judgment told her. After all, some idle gossip overheard in a hospital lobby couldn't change your life. It was just — words. But she really and truly didn't know. She needed facts, she needed truth, and when she confronted Mrs. LaBurge she would know if she was lying . . .

A car came down Harrison Street and stopped in front of the house. Lukie recognized one of the Eastern Star ladies in the driver's seat. Mrs. LaBurge got out and hurried up the walk. Lukie stepped out from under the catalpa tree and was about to call to her when a flash of lightning lit up the sky and illuminated Mrs. LaBurge's face with an eerie clarity — the sunken eyes, the fleshy cheeks, the slack mouth. The rain had smeared her make-up, like oils washing from some grotesque painting. Lukie stopped dead in her tracks. What a hideous woman! she thought. Quickly, she turned and fled, through the backyard and down to Elm Street. It was as if she had seen the face of evil, and she knew beyond a shadow of a doubt that Beatrice LaBurge had lied.

Mr. Seed was checking a proof of the final four-page run of the paper when Lukie got down to the *Clarion* office. A bottle of bourbon was sitting on the desk. Lukie glanced over his shoulder.

3 DIE, 26 INJURED IN HIGBIE BLAST!
Farnsworth E. Bishop, of "Buttermilk
Twins" Fame, Among Fatalities

And at the bottom of the page, another story:

CIVIC LEADERS PLEDGE SUPPORT
OF HOSPITAL FUND DRIVE

Mr. Seed lit a cigar and propped his feet up on the desk.

"It's been one of those days you wish you'd taken up carpentry," he said.

He uncorked the bottle and took a swig from it.

"It's funny how things work out, Lukie. Three men die, and because of it a hospital will be built, and many other men will live. Round and round she goes, and where she stops nobody knows."

Lukie took off her slicker and sat down in one of the swivel chairs. The rumble of the big flat-bed press came from the back shop.

"I suppose you're aware," Mr. Seed said, "that I heard that nasty remark Beatrice made over at the hospital last night."

"Yes, sir," Lukie replied. "I figured you did."

"Have you had time to think it over?"

"Yes, sir."

"And have you reached a conclusion?"

"Yes, sir," Lukie said firmly. "She was lying."

Mr. Seed smiled and nodded.

"I knew you wouldn't go off the deep end," he said.

He puffed thoughtfully on his cigar for a moment, then added, "You know, there isn't much that escapes a small-town editor, so I'm going to tell you something that only two other people in town know. Your Uncle Farnie couldn't have had children."

Lukie looked up sharply at Mr. Seed.

"He was hurt in the war," the editor went on. "He couldn't have had a normal marriage."

"You said two other people know?"

"Your mother and father. Who else?"

And suddenly it all fell into place — Uncle Farnie's lack of ambition, his drinking and his melancholy and his aimless flirtations with the mill girls. And the heartbreak of Reenie Axford, the girl with the mittened hand — a love that could not be.

"Gossip is a vicious thing, Lukie," Mr. Seed said. "After a while it assumes a life of its own. Beatrice spread that story around the year you were born. Everybody knew Walter and Farnie had fought like dogs over your mother, and so there was just enough truth in it to make it seem plausible."

"But how could she do such a thing now," Lukie asked, "with Uncle Farnie dead?"

"Hell hath no fury," Mr. Seed quoted in reply. "Years back she had a crush on Farnie, but he wouldn't give her the time of day."

170

"Is that what kept my father and Uncle Farnie apart all those years — my mother?"

"To begin with, I suppose. But later on they argued over the estate, and after that I think it was just plain stubbornness. Pity! In their heyday, they were a pair; yes, sir, a real legend. You think Billy Butts had razzle-dazzle? You should've seen the Buttermilk Twins in action."

The rumble of the flat-bed press had stopped. The office was quiet except for the ticking of the big wall clock. They sat in silence for a few moments, and then Mr. Seed got to his feet.

"Well . . ." He sighed wearily. "We'd best get at the folding."

He took Lukie's hand and held it for a moment.

"I was proud of the way you held together today, young lady. It wasn't easy, was it?"

"No, sir," Lukie said, forcing a little smile. "But I had a lot of help."

Two days later, Uncle Farnie was laid to rest, at the edge of a grassy knoll in the cemetery. It was one of the biggest funerals the town had ever seen. The fire company was there, and just about everybody from Higbie's, as well as Uncle Farnie's cronies from the tap room. A Legion bugler blew Taps as the casket was lowered into the ground, and afterward everyone came up to Walter and Myrene Bishop and had a kind word.

"Golly," Buddy said as they were leaving the cemetery, "Uncle Farnie must've had a lot of friends."

"Yes, Buddy," Lukie replied. "He had an awful lot of friends."

Lukie altered her customary route to school so that she went by Uncle Farnie's grave. Frequently, on her way home, she sat by the headstone, remembering. He'd given her so much love and joy and laughter, and after a while the hurt started to go away.

28

The planes came in over Zebron Falls out of the west, a whole squadron of them, in precise military formation.

"You don't suppose we're going to be bombed," Sally said nervously. The first bell had just rung, and she and Lukie were hurrying up the steps of the high school. "I mean, maybe Mr. Panella was right."

Mr. Panella was already up in the bell tower, consulting his aircraft recognition manual.

"P–Forty-seven Thunderbolts!" he called down. Students and teachers were hurrying out on the lawn to catch a glimpse of the planes. "Army fighters. They're probably on some kind of training exercise."

But above South Hill, the formation banked steeply and began circling the town. Then one of the planes peeled off in a straight run on the high school.

"It's Billy!" Mr. Panella shouted, peering through his binoculars. "I can see him plain as day!"

The Thunderbolt roared over the school at treetop level, the barrels of its wing guns glinting in the morning sun. Windows rattled, and the ground seemed to vibrate. Lukie looked up, and there was Billy — unmistakably Billy — in a helmet and goggles, grinning and waving. Students scurried about everywhere, waving back. Lukie dropped her books and started jumping up and down.

"Hello, Billy!" she shouted, running across the lawn to keep him in sight. "Hel-lo!"

And then the plane soared up over the river, its silver wings rocking in salute, and was gone. Lukie could scarcely contain herself. Billy Butts a fighter pilot! Somehow, she thought with a bursting pride, he had taken on the entire U.S. Army — and had won.

"Do you think he's an officer?" Sally asked excitedly. "Pilots are always officers, aren't they? Oh, I just can't believe it!"

An hour later, Lukie was summoned from Homeroom.

"You have a visitor," Mr. Severence explained.

It was Mr. Butts, in overalls and a straw hat, his normally serious face beaming with a broad smile. Billy had just phoned, he said, from Selfridge Field, north of Detroit. His squadron was being shipped overseas — to England, probably, where an invasion buildup was in progress — but would remain overnight at Selfridge, awaiting the arrival of another fighter group. Billy's commanding officer had given him permission to come home. He would be on the 7:55 local that evening.

"Oh, yes," Mr. Butts added, "Junior will be with him."

Lukie felt her heart leap. Billy and Junior were coming home — and it was prom night!

"Junior is on his way to the Pacific," Mr. Butts said. "It seems the two of them have been cooking up this little surprise for several weeks."

And so that night, at the senior prom, the youngsters of the Tuesday Musicale, who had shared so much together, were reunited for the last time. The girls looked radiant in their organdy gowns and white sandals, with corsages of ribboned gardenias and little sequined purses, which they gave to the boys to carry in their pockets. Miss Pray and Mr. Panella hurried over from the chaperones' section when they saw Billy and Junior.

"Billy!" Miss Pray smiled proudly, taking each of them by the hand. "Junior!"

She stood back to look at them — Billy in his gabardine second lieutenant's uniform, and Junior, tanned and confident, in dress blues, with a pair of silver wings gleaming from his chest.

"Why, you're grown men!" she said in amazement.

And then she gathered them all around her in one great hug — Billy and Junior, Sally and Lukie.

"All my children!" She smiled, her eyes filling with tears. "You've been a burst of sunshine in my life! Such joy, such treasure, and now it's ending!"

And then the gym was filled with sweet music, and the rustle of dresses, and the laughter of gay young voices. The creaky old gymnasium had been decorated in a springlike motif of lavender and white, with arbors and trellises and a little picket fence around the bandstand. Harvey's orchestra had come over from Ann Arbor — but with a substitute pianist.

"Harvey has a violin recital tonight," Lukie explained to Billy. "It's very important. Some professors from a conservatory in Boston are going to be there."

Billy held court around the punch bowl, telling of his meteoric rise from waiter to fighter pilot.

"So when I got to New York, I just kept on going, to Washington, and camped outside General Marshall's office . . ."

"General *George* Marshall!" Sally said in astonishment. "The Army Chief of *Staff*!"

"Uh-huh." Billy grinned. "I figured I might as well go straight to the top."

He had sat there for three days, he said, ignoring pointed suggestions from secretaries and adjutants and miscellaneous brass that he go away. Finally, just as his furlough was about to run out, General Marshall himself had come out and summoned Billy into his office.

"Well, we had brandy and cigars, and then I propped my feet up on the desk and said, 'Now lookee here, George' — We were on a first-name basis by then — 'Lookee here, you can get any dull ol' white boy to serve up gin rickeys down at Maxwell Field, but you're looking at the president of the Zebron High Student Council . . .' "

Addison Carey, in a white jacket and tuxedo trousers, doubled up in laughter.

"Well, ol' George looked at me for a minute, then said, 'By cracky, Billy, you're right!' Then he pressed a buzzer, and all these adjutants came scurrying in, and right on the spot they wrote me out orders for a new all-Negro fighter wing that was being trained down in Texas. Four hours later, I was on my way to Randolph Field."

"But, Billy," Sally said, "why didn't you let anyone know you were a flight cadet? Your parents were worried sick."

"It would've been worse," Billy replied, "to get their hopes up and then have me flunk out."

And then the orchestra struck up a loud fanfare. The crowd began moving toward the bandstand.

"It's the 'Sweetheart Waltz,' " Lukie said, taking Billy's hand. "Sally's going to win for sure."

It was a tradition at Zebron High for seniors to vote on the most popular girl of the graduating class, who was then designated Class Sweetheart and given the honor of leading the "Sweetheart Waltz" at the prom. Lukie and Lorena Pearsall had campaigned hard for Sally, even putting up heart-shaped placards in the Main Hall.

Addison Carey, clowning around as usual, acted as master of ceremonies and made a big production out of opening the envelope that contained the name of the winner.

"And the Sweetheart of the Class of Forty-four is . . . none other than . . . your friend and mine . . ."

The crowd groaned in suspense.

"Lukie Bishop!"

There was a loud rolling of drums. A blue spotlight shone on Lukie, who stood there dumfounded. Sally and Lorena began jumping up and down.

177

"We did it behind your back, Lukie!" Sally cried happily. "It was unanimous!"

Lukie's mind was all awhirl — the smiling faces, the cheers, the applause. Her eyes filled with tears and her lips began to quiver, and for a moment she was once again the shy, gangling girl who had wanted to run away from home to avoid going to high school.

"Go *on*, Lukie!" Sally nudged her.

The orchestra was playing a lovely waltz. A quartet from the *a cappella* choir sang the lyrics. A hush came over the crowd as they waited expectantly for the Class Sweetheart to choose her partner. Lukie rubbed the tears from her eyes and turned to Billy.

"Lieutenant Butts," she said demurely, making a little curtsy.

"Miss Bishop," Billy acknowledged, bowing.

Lukie went into Billy's arms, and the two of them glided out onto the floor. The crowd made a circle as they swept round and round, Lukie's head flung back and her eyes all aglow.

> *In the shadows let me come and sing to you,*
> *In the shadows let me bring the spring to you . . .*

Then the other couples began dancing, Sally and Junior, Miss Pray and Mr. Panella. And Lukie knew that for the rest of her life, whenever she looked back on her senior year at Zebron High, this was the moment she would remember.

> *Love's old song will be new,*
> *In the shadows when I come and sing to you.*

29

After the prom, in the moonlight, Lukie Bishop and Billy Butts walked down to the river.

"Your Uncle Farnie was right," Billy said, gazing up at the stars. "It's the best sky in the world. Let's go up to your secret hiding place. I'll bet we could see all the way to Canada."

"It isn't mine anymore," Lukie said. She gathered up the hem of her gown to keep it from getting wet in the dew. "I gave it to Buddy."

"Too bad. We had some fine times up there."

"Yes, we did, didn't we?" Lukie smiled. "Remember the time I fell off the bluff?"

"Remember?" Billy grinned. "How could I forget? I thought you were dead. Do you still have the scar?"

Lukie took Billy's hand and tilted her head forward. "Feel," she said.

179

Billy ran his fingers through her hair till he located a long, thin welt.

"It only shows when the wind blows my hair," Lukie said — and noticed that her knees were trembling.

"It's funny, isn't it," Billy said, rubbing the scar, "how certain places are only good for certain times, and then when those times are over it's different?"

They walked down through the orchard to their fishing spot — the dead elm that had fallen into the river. Billy spread out his gabardine tunic for Lukie to sit on.

"Oh, Billy," Lukie said, "it's been so hard with you gone."

She told him about Lady and the orchard and the explosion — and about Harvey.

"You and Harvey . . ." Billy asked hesitantly, "is it serious?"

"I don't know, Billy." Lukie sighed. "Sometimes I think I ought to marry him; that I owe it to him."

"Because of his eyes?"

"Yes. But I won't if you tell me not to. Only you've got to tell me, Billy. Once I make the commitment I won't back out."

She took his hand and held it to her cheek.

"It's not just brother and sister with us, Billy. You know that, don't you?"

Billy looked down at the river and then at Lukie. A sadness came into his eyes.

"Yes, Lukie," he said. "I guess I've always known it. That's what kept me going when things got rough down at Randolph Field, thinking of you and imagining — things."

Lukie slipped into Billy's arms.

"Oh, Billy, you don't have to imagine anything," she murmured, her eyes glistening in the moonlight. "We've got tonight, and then after the war we'll make a special life for ourselves, a private life. We'll make love up in the loft and go away on trips. Nobody will ever know the difference."

Billy shook his head.

"It's no good, Lukie. People would kill it."

"But I don't care about people, Billy!"

"Yes, you do, Lukie," Billy insisted. "What if something went wrong? Lukie Bishop with a mulatto hidden away in the attic — is that what you want?"

"Then we'll go someplace else."

"What would that change? We'd just end up hating each other. Besides, you could never leave Zebron Falls, Lukie. You're as much a part of the town as the river and the valley and the sky above it."

"But so are you, Billy."

"I don't know, Lukie," Billy said. "There are all kinds of things I don't know, about myself and my family and how come we're fighting a war for democracy with an army that makes Negroes do all the dirty work. But I know one thing — if my father can achieve what he has in Zebron Falls, then a lot of other colored people can achieve it, if everybody would just get out of their way."

He told her about the changes that had occurred in his thinking, and as he talked Lukie sensed the futility of their situation. He had seen much misery and oppression, he said, and he couldn't turn his back on it.

"The guys in my squadron say I'm like a chocolate

marshmallow cookie," he said, "brown on the outside and white on the inside. And they're right, Lukie. Growing up in Zebron Falls I was a white boy who just happened to be colored. And so I'm going to darken up my insides a little."

"But what will you do, Billy?"

"My commanding officer used to be a professor at a Negro university in Washington. When the war's over, I'm going to enroll there and study law. Things will be happening, important things, and I want to be ready . . ."

"Oh, Billy, let me go with you!" Lukie implored him. "Please let me go with you! We could get swallowed up in a big city like that . . ."

"No, Lukie, no! You can't share it. Don't you under- stand? It's my fight, and you can't share it."

"But you'll go away and never come back."

Billy lifted Lukie's head and brushed the tears from her cheeks. "No, Lukie," he said gently, "I'll always come back to Zebron Falls. You'll be here."

They talked long into the night. A gossamer mist rose from the river and enveloped them, muffling their voices and shutting out the night, until it seemed they were drifting on a cloud, timeless and lovely. Billy told Lukie many things, things that made her laugh and things that made her cry, as if he were cramming into one brief in- terlude a courtship that could not be. When it was time for him to leave, Lukie clung to him and didn't want to let go.

"It was wonderful growing up together," she whispered in the orchard, "wasn't it, Billy?"

"Yes, Lukie," Billy answered, a crack in his voice. "I

182

guess it was the most wonderful thing in the world."

Later, in her bedroom, Lukie undressed in the dark, then curled up in the dormer windowseat, in her long polka dot nightgown. She looked wistfully out toward Great Oaks. Only two summers ago, she thought, Billy and Junior had practiced laterals in the south pasture. Now they were going off to war, and nothing would be the same again.

And as she sat at the window, alone with her memories, she reached in the dark for the gooseneck lamp on the desk. She switched the lamp on and off several times, then waited. In a moment, a light flashed in the night from Billy's window, flickering through the Lombardy poplars, once, twice, three times —

And then it went out.

Part Four

30

On the eve of exam week, Mr. Severence called a special assembly of the senior class. The class was within a grade point, he told them, of topping the school scholastic record, which had been established in 1889.

"It won't be easy," he warned them. "Your teachers will be tough. We don't give out good grades lightly at Zebron High. But if you set your minds to it, you can do it."

And so as the days grew balmy and the lilacs came into bloom, the Class of '44 buckled down to make its mark. All that week, the school remained opened till nine at night. Teachers gave up their free time to work with students who required help. A serious mood filled the halls, and there was less horseplay between classes.

"Such decorum," remarked Mr. Panella. "It seems abnormal."

One evening, as Lukie and Addison Carey were cramming logarithms in the study hall, Mr. Leiber, beaming with excitement, signaled from the doorway. Lukie hurried out into the hall. Harvey had been offered a full scholarship to the conservatory in Boston, Mr. Leiber reported, plus a supplemental grant that would cover any special requirements arising from his failing eyesight.

"How wonderful!" Lukie cried.

"But — there is a problem," he cautioned. "Harvey isn't sure he will accept."

"Not accept?" Lukie said, baffled. "But it's the opportunity he's always dreamed of."

"I know, I know," Mr. Leiber answered, "but he says he is reluctant to leave Zebron Falls; that it is the only real home he has ever known."

As Mr. Leiber talked, Lukie sensed that she was the cause of Harvey's indecision. She had felt an obligation to him. Did he now feel an obligation to her?

"There is very little time," Mr. Leiber went on. "Harvey has been invited to Boston to visit the school. They are hoping he will stay for the summer term. We are leaving the day before graduation."

"We?" Lukie asked.

"Yes. I have friends in Boston. I hope to stay a week or so until Harvey gets settled. Talk to him, Lukie. You have great influence with him. Help him to make the right decision."

"Yes, sir," Lukie promised. "I'll try."

"It is curious," Mr. Leiber added, almost as an afterthought, "but Harvey's blindness may very well assure his concert career."

"I don't understand."

"But of course. Without his disability, a scholarship of this magnitude would be out of the question. It is a quirk of fate."

That night, Lukie started to call Harvey in Ann Arbor, but when the operator came on the line she was filled with confusion and hung up the phone. She needed time to think. Mr. Leiber had said they would be making the trip to Boston regardless. She would put off talking to Harvey till after exams.

And exactly what would she have Harvey do? Whatever was right for him — yes, but would that be right for *her*? She knew she could never bring herself to leave Zebron Falls and follow him to the conservatory. And yet if he stayed, would it be any different? He lived in a world that was shut off to her, would always be shut off. More important, it would be a long time before she forgot those moments with Billy beside the river.

There was a trap in going with just one boy, she was discovering. The town got used to the idea, felt comfortable with it, and pressured you to keep it that way. And so you went together, and one thing led to another until finally you got married. She wondered how many people in town had gotten married not out of love but because of habit. But it didn't have to be that way. You didn't have to marry a boy just out of habit — or obligation.

A quirk of fate, Mr. Leiber had said. Was she, was everyone, an instrument in some vast plan? A boy gets knocked over a dam in a little town in Michigan and as a result brings great beauty to the lives of people all over the world. How fragile life was! She thought of that day

189

at the swimming pond. If she and Billy hadn't ridden the North Star, or if Junior hadn't dunked her, or if Harvey hadn't been sitting on the guard rail — the millions and trillions of causes and effects that had put them in precisely that place at precisely that moment —

Finally, exams were over. Half the senior class gathered in the Main Hall to await the results. It was late afternoon when Mr. Severence emerged from his office — smiling.

"This is the most satisfying moment of my career," he said. "My deepest congratulations to the Class of Forty-four. You have just made history."

An ear-splitting roar echoed through the halls. "To the Sweet Shoppe!" somebody yelled, and an avalanche of joyous students burst from the school.

"Oh, I just can't wait to write Junior!" cried Sally.

Dark clouds were moving in from the southwest when Lukie finally got home. The house was deserted; it was Friday, her mother's day at Red Cross. She went up to her room and flopped on the bed with her clothes on, exhausted. She slept straight through supper and a severe thunderstorm and her favorite radio programs. She was still sleeping at ten o'clock, when the phone rang.

It was Mrs. DeBaene. Would Lukie please come right over? Junior Rosenquist had been killed. His plane had crashed at sea during naval maneuvers off the California coast, and Sally was beside herself.

31

And so it was Sally — lovely, guileless Sally, at the eager beginning of a new life — who was the first to be hurt by the war.

Lukie got dressed and put on her slicker and hurried over to the DeBaenes' house on Taylor Street. Sally was waiting out on the porch, sitting on the steps, with her arms wrapped around her knees.

"Sally?" Lukie said cautiously. "Are you all right?"

"Yes." Sally nodded. Her eyes seemed oddly bright and alert. "I suppose I shouldn't be, but it's the weirdest thing, Lukie; I feel all keyed up. My whole body. I mean, my senses have never been so sharp, and the most incredible thoughts keep flying through my head — really brilliant."

"How did you hear about Junior?"

"Mrs. Rosenquist called. They sent her a telegram.

191

Oh, Lukie, stay with me tonight. I'll go bats if I don't have someone to talk to."

"Ask your mother if you can come over to our place," Lukie said. "We'll sleep in the loft."

It was a black night. There were deep rumbles of thunder, and the glow of lightning rippled across the sky. The girls walked in the rain for what seemed hours.

"Maybe he really isn't dead," Sally said. "Junior always had something up his sleeve. Maybe he's drifting on a raft, or something. A telegram doesn't *prove* anything. I mean, people aren't dead till you see them in their caskets."

She had been thinking about death a lot, Sally said, ever since Junior enlisted — in bed, with the house dark, and the sounds of the night coming in the window. She couldn't imagine any of them dying, although she knew one day they would. One night she had thought of the homecoming game and the way Junior had looked when he scored the winning touchdown. It had seemed so real, as if she could reach out and touch it, and she wondered where it had gone.

"I mean, you do something — you sing in the May Festival, or go to the prom, or spend a week at Clam Lake — and then it's over and done with. But where does it *go*?"

They walked in silence through the murky night. The rain had abated to a thin drizzle. As they cut through the cemetery, a flash of lightning lit up the little flags and piles of wilted flowers left from Decoration Day. How little we know about people, Lukie thought. She wanted to comfort Sally, but could think of nothing to say. Instead, she told her about her plan for the orchard.

"In a couple of years there might be enough money for regular jobs," she said. "It would be so good for you, Sally, and we'd be sticking together."

"Oh, Lukie," Sally said wearily, "you can't keep your brood around you forever. Besides, I'll go crazy if I don't get out of this — burg. At least for a while. It's different with you. You see the town as some great poem, but all I see is dreary little people leading dreary little lives, and for what? I know I shouldn't feel that way. I love Zebron Falls, and it will always be my town, but — oh, I don't know."

"But where will you go, Sally?" Lukie asked.

"To live with my aunt, just the way I'd planned. Mr. Panella promised to write a letter of recommendation to the theater group. Junior said you have to make your life count for your own sake, and so I guess I'll go to Chicago and see if there's anything in me worth counting. The only thing is, it will be so — lonely."

Sally's voice began to break. "Oh, Lukie, is he really dead?"

"Yes, Sally," Lukie answered, her eyes beginning to fill. "He's really dead."

And finally the tears came. Sally crumpled up against Lukie in great, wracking sobs.

"He wanted me to go all the way with him the night of the prom. I wish I had. Oh, how I wish I had!"

Lukie had already brought fresh linens and candles out to the loft. It was very late when Sally finally cried herself to sleep. Lukie sat with her for a while to make sure she was sleeping soundly. Next week would be their final week at Zebron High, she thought — the class play, baccalaureate services, commencement, and then it would all be over. She had wanted it to be a time of sweeping triumphs, especially for Sally, and now —

She set her alarm for six o'clock but was awake before it went off. Sally was still sleeping. She went to the window. The rain had stopped, and the sun was trying to break through the morning mist. Make your life count for your own sake, Junior had said. She looked down over her vegetable garden. Her sweet corn had sprouted, little green spears in neat rows. It would be a fine growing year; she could always tell. She would set out her tomato plants today and fork in the rotted manure Mr. Butts had given her for her asparagus bed. It would be good in the garden; it was always good in the garden.

And in that moment, Lukie reached a decision. She wasn't cut out to be a virtuoso's wife or a nurse or even a teacher at Zebron High.

She was a farmer.

32

Sally's debut in *The Importance of Being Earnest* was a great success. For two golden hours, the ingénue, Cecily, came to life in the darkened gymnasium with a sparkle that kept the audience enthralled. It was as if Sally, in her Victorian costume and carrying a pink parasol, was immersing herself in a make-believe world in order to shut out her grief over Junior. When it was over there were seven curtain calls. "Bravo! Bravo!" called Miss Pray, and Mr. Panella rushed onstage with a basket of roses.

But at baccalaureate services the next night, at St. Philip's, Sally broke down during the memorial service for Junior and had to be led from the chapel. The school had written to the Navy for transcripts of Junior's military training, Mr. Severence disclosed, in hopes of posthumously awarding him a diploma.

"Junior Rosenquist was a credit to his school and to his country," he said. "It would be a small token of our esteem."

When the Honor Society awards were announced, Lukie learned that she had placed third in her class, a fraction of a point behind Addison Carey and Lorena Pearsall. After the ceremony, Mr. Severence took her aside.

"I was hoping you would be our valedictorian," he said. "If you hadn't spent so much time helping the others cram for exams — well, I know it would have been different."

Lukie, feeling very self-assured in her maize and blue cap and gown, was not at all dismayed.

"But we broke the record, didn't we?" She smiled brightly. "Besides, being Class Sweetheart and valedictorian, too, would have been — pushy."

On the day before graduation, Harvey arrived home with barely enough time to catch his train to Boston. For a while, Lukie was afraid they'd have no time alone, but finally they managed to slip away from the news agency for a walk.

"Your father is so funny," Lukie said. "He's more nervous about your leaving than you are."

"It's a big event for him." Harvey laughed. "He's already inviting his friends to my debut at Carnegie Hall."

It was a warm spring afternoon. They walked up South Hill to Eberline's pasture. Harvey seemed very relaxed. There was none of the temperament that had characterized his behavior over the past six months, and Lukie wondered if he, too, had reached a decision.

"You've just got to accept that scholarship, Harvey," she said. "It would be sinful not to. You've got to forget what I said last Christmas and do what's right for you."

"Yes, I'm going to," Harvey agreed. "I've been doing a lot of thinking, Lukie. It may sound dumb, but I don't care about being blind. I mean, if I had to choose between my eyes and my music, I'd choose my music. I don't think I could live without it."

"It isn't dumb, Harvey. It's beautiful."

They cut over to the top of the pasture, where there was a view of the town and the valley and the river. The church spires gleamed in the bright afternoon sun.

"Remember the day of your accident, Harvey?" Lukie said.

"Remember? How could I forget?"

"Well — I was the one who knocked you into the dam."

"Yes, I know."

"You do!" Lukie stared at him in amazement.

"I saw you out of the corner of my eye," Harvey said with a smile.

"But you never said anything to the lifeguard."

"What for? You didn't do it on purpose, did you?"

"Oh, Harvey!" Lukie sighed. "And all these years I've felt so terrible about it."

"Is that why you wanted to sell the orchard and have us get married?"

"I guess so," Lukie admitted. "Not entirely, but that was part of it. And you . . . Were you going to turn down the scholarship because of me?"

"Yes."

A little shiver ran through Lukie. "Golly, it's scary,

isn't it?" she said. "We nearly wrecked each other's lives with our good intentions. Are you angry with me?"

"Of course not, silly," Harvey said. "You're the best thing that's ever happened to me."

"Oh, Harvey, do you really mean that? Because you've been so good for me. I mean, I was just a wallflower, and then we started going together and I discovered things about myself I never knew existed."

"And now it's over?" Harvey asked.

"Yes," Lukie answered, her eyes moist. "I guess it never really got started. It was just my stupid determination to barge in and run your life." She paused for a moment, then asked, "And you? Is it over for you, Harvey?"

"No, not over. It's just become something else. I don't know, but it seems that when you reach certain milestones in your life you start putting things into perspective. You're more important to me as a friend, Lukie, than as a sweetheart."

"Thank you, Harvey," Lukie said softly. "That was a lovely thing to say."

A train whistle echoed from up the valley. Another train to be caught, Lukie thought resentfully. It seemed her life had become nothing but train whistles and depots.

"We'd better get back," Harvey said. "I've got to help Dad with the luggage."

He pulled Lukie to her feet, and they started out of the pasture.

"You haven't said anything about yourself, Lukie,"

Harvey said. "What are your plans for next year?"

"I've decided to go to college."

"Ann Arbor, I suppose."

"No."

She told him about her plan for the orchard — the cider mill and the store and the fruit farm.

"It will require a lot of background," she said. "So I'm going to register at Michigan State and study agriculture. I've already sent for an application."

"The cow college!" Harvey exclaimed, elated. "But of course. It's so — *you*."

"Yes, I suppose it is." Lukie smiled. "I'll just go to classes and study hard and let things happen."

"Yes," Harvey agreed. "I guess that's what life is all about. You just jump in and let things happen."

"Why, Harvey Toles!" Lukie declared. "You're a regular philosopher!"

Mr. Toles, in his old tweed jacket with the leather-patched elbows, had stacked Harvey's bags in the wooden newspaper cart. Sally was waiting for them at the depot, and Mr. Leiber — in a checked double-breasted suit and carrying a worn gripsack.

"It was my traveling bag with the Detroit Symphony." He smiled proudly. "It has been halfway around the world — Budapest, even."

There was a rush of handshakes and goodbyes as the train pulled in.

"I'll take good care of the virtuoso, Mr. Toles!" Mr. Leiber called to Harvey's father. "We will dine at Locke-Ober's and walk in the Common!"

199

Lukie held back till last.

"Well, goodbye, Harvey," she said, hugging him tight. "Take good care of yourself."

"You know something?" Harvey grinned. "We ought to break up more often. I think we're better friends than before."

"We'll always be good friends, Harvey." Lukie kissed him lightly on the lips. "Will you still come back to Zebron Falls when you're a famous violinist?"

"I'll always come back to Zebron Falls, Lukie," Harvey answered. "You'll be here."

Lukie looked at him quizzically.

"That's funny," she said. "That's what Billy said."

Harvey and Mr. Leiber waved through the window as the train went down the tracks. Mr. Toles shook his head sadly.

"The train isn't even out of sight," he said, "and already I'm missing him. But — we go where life leads us."

He sighed and put his arms around Lukie and Sally.

"Well, young ladies, this has been a sad week for all of us. But there will be good days and there will be bad days, and great is Mother Russia."

"Chekhov!" Lukie laughed.

"Correct." Mr. Toles nodded approvingly. "I see they teach you something besides home economics at that school."

They started up the platform toward Main Street.

"Come, my little rabbits. We will drown our sorrows at the Sweet Shoppe and talk of the old days."

33

Commencement day dawned fresh and lovely. A soft lilac glow filled the horizon. It had rained in the night, but now the sky was clear and blue and cloudless.

Lukie was awake with the birds. She stretched and yawned and listened to the sounds of the morning. This was her day. This day would never come again — and she thought of the sampler above the blackboard in Mr. Panella's room: "Today is the first day of the rest of your life."

"Lukie!" It was Myrene Bishop calling up from downstairs. "I'm gong to need some more thread to finish hemming your dress!"

"All right, Mama," Lukie called back. "I'll run down to Mitzelfeld's after breakfast."

Beth and Buddy were leaving for school when Lukie came down to breakfast — only the seniors had completed their classes — and Walter Bishop had already left for the mill.

"How come Daddy left for work so early?" Lukie asked her mother.

"The Navy inspectors are coming today," Myrene Bishop answered — and added cautiously, "He might be a little late tonight, dear."

"Oh, fine!" Lukie groaned. "On my graduation day, of all days!"

She had a premonition of disaster. He wouldn't show up, she thought. What he said in the orchard was just talk. He wouldn't show up, just as Uncle Farnie had never shown up, and it would be spoiled.

"Now don't work yourself into a pet, dear," her mother said. "He'll be there. He promised faithfully."

Lukie decided to walk into town rather than take her bike. The larkspur was in bloom. Sparrows chittered in the trellises. As she went by the high school, the custodians were setting up chairs out on the tennis courts, where the commencement exercises would be held. It was a perfect day for graduation, she thought, and she felt her spirits improving. But when she saw the newsstand in front of Crissman's Drugs, her heart sank.

ALLIES INVADE NORMANDY!

She stared at the headline as if transfixed. Normandy? Where was *Nor*mandy? The strange places they picked to have battles. Oh, Billy! She thought.

She finished her errands and hurried home. A wave of self-pity came over her. It was as if there were a conspiracy to ruin her graduation — and immediately she felt guilty about her selfish thoughts. There had been many casualties, the paper had said, and the beaches were red with blood.

The day flew by in a whirl. Lukie and her mother worked feverishly, preparing for the open-house. There were floors to be scrubbed, lemons to be squeezed, cakes to be baked. One chore led to another till it seemed they would never finish.

"Oh, Mama," Lukie said impatiently, "there'll never be enough time to finish my dress!"

Finally, Beth and Buddy straggled home from school and were put to work, polishing the silver and washing the big bay windows. Myrene Bishop got Lukie's graduation dress from the front hall closet and took it to the sunroom.

"Not too short, Mama." Lukie stood on the little wicker footstool while her mother marked the hem. "My knees will look knobby if it's too short."

It was a lovely, summery dress — a shirtwaist of white dotted Swiss, with a full skirt and little tucks in the bodice.

"Hold still, dear," Myrene Bishop mumbled through a mouthful of pins. "You're as nervous as a June bride."

Lukie found herself growing tense and irritable. Beth and Buddy kept running in and pestering her. Five o'clock came and went, with no sign of her father.

"*Lu*kie! Stop fidgeting!"

"Oh, Mama, I can't help it! It's all wrong. It's not the way I thought it was going to be."

"Now, now, dear," her mother said soothingly, "everything will be just fine. Graduations have a way of taking care of themselves."

And she reminisced about her own graduation. Grandpa Axford had thrown a party for the entire class, she said — at the St. James Hotel, with flowers and a buffet supper and an orchestra with three saxophones.

"The boys were going off to war then, too," she said, and smiled. "Your Uncle Farnie poured a bottle of gin in the punch bowl."

"Did he really?" Lukie giggled. "I'll bet Grandpa Axford had a fit."

"No," her mother replied, "he just sampled the punch and said, 'Well, if they're old enough to die in the trenches, they're old enough to drink spiked punch.' "

Her eyes misted up.

"We sang 'Auld Lang Syne' and promised to hold reunions every year."

"And did you?" Lukie asked.

"Oh, at first. But things happen; you lose touch."

"It won't be that way with our crowd," Lukie said firmly. "We're going to stick together forever."

Myrene Bishop got to her feet and placed her hands on Lukie's shoulders.

"Oh, Lukie." A sadness came into her eyes. "If only there were some way of preparing you. You think it won't be the same, but it will. It has already started. Half the boys will be in uniform before the end of summer. Sally will be leaving for Chicago, and . . ."

"That's just because she's upset over Junior," Lukie declared. "She'll be back."

"No, Lukie, no!" Myrene Bishop looked searchingly

into her daughter's eyes. "Sally's world is changing, can't you see? And so is yours. Don't try to hang on to it. Let it go, dear, let it go . . ."

The doorbell rang. There was a clatter of feet as Beth ran to answer it.

"Lukie, come quick!" she yelled. "It's a package!"

Lukie raced to the front hall, barefoot, her dress unfastened at the back. She returned, carrying a tiny jeweler's box.

"It's from Billy," she said excitedly. "He told Mr. Lake not to deliver it till graduation day."

She curled up on the footstool, pins sticking from the hem of her dress, and opened the box. It was a gold locket, cameo-shaped, with an amethyst set in the center.

"There's an inscription," she said, and as she held the locket up to the light to read it, she burst uncontrollably into tears.

June 6, 1944
In my heart, always.
Billy

"Oh, Mama" she said through her sobs, "I feel as if my heart's breaking in two!"

Myrene Bishop dropped to her knees and took her daughter into her arms.

"There, there, dear," she said, cradling Lukie to her bosom. "The hurt will go away."

"No, Mama, no," Lukie murmured. "Something's been cut out of me . . ."

And then the sobbing stopped. Slowly, Lukie looked up at her mother.

"Mama, you *know?*" she said, wide-eyed.

"Yes." Myrene Bishop smiled. "I saw the two of you in the orchard prom night. But I think I knew it even before you did, watching you tag after Billy like a kid sister and sensing that one day it would stop being brother and sister and become something else."

"Oh, Mama, it hurts so bad."

"I know, dear," her mother said. "Oh, yes, I know."

"Was it that way with you and Uncle Farnie?"

"Oh-h?" Myrene Bishop raised an eyebrow. "So you figured that out, did you? Well, your Uncle Farnsworth and I shared some happy memories. But understand me, Lukie — if I had it to do over, I wouldn't change a thing." She mussed up Lukie's hair. "Besides, I wouldn't have had you, would I?"

She pulled Lukie to her feet.

"We'll have a long talk tomorrow, dear. Now run up and get your cap and gown and let's see how they look with your dress."

Lukie dried her eyes and clung to her mother for a moment.

"Thank you, Mama," she whispered. "Thank you for everything."

Myrene Bishop held her daughter close.

"Do me proud tonight, Lukie," she said gently. "You're my first and my dearest. Do me proud."

34

And then sadly, sweetly — it came to an end.

The sun was dipping behind the trees as the Class of '44, filled with a sense of the solemnity of the occasion, marched slowly down the high school lawn to the tennis courts. The choir began singing the Alma Mater.

> *"O Zebron Falls! we sing thy praises,*
> *As twilight's silence falls.*
> *Thy flame of truth e'er shall guide us,*
> *Beyond these hallowed halls."*

The color guard moved up the center aisle, bearing the Stars and Stripes, flanked by the state flag and the maize and blue Zebron High banner. Lukie searched the crowd anxiously for her family, but in vain. And then she saw them, hurrying around the bank of lilac bushes behind the speakers' platform, her father in the lead and Buddy struggling with an unlaced shoe. Beth and Buddy spotted her and waved. Buddy crossed his eyes and made a face, and Lukie quickly bent her head to conceal her grin.

Mr. Higbie gave the commencement address.

"The Class of Forty-four is special. You are special because of your scholastic achievements, and you are special because of the great uncertainties that confront you in a war-torn world . . ."

He spoke in deep, sonorous tones—of honor and pride, truth and integrity. And as the words rang out over the audience, an evening breeze fluttered the state flag, with its Latin motto: *Si quaeris peninsulum amoenam circumspice.* If you seek a pleasant peninsula, look about you.

"And so as you go out into the mainstream of life . . ."

Lukie's attention wandered. It was all so misleading, she thought. They had been in the mainstream of life ever since they drew their first breath, sharing its joys and sorrows, accepting its risks. She gazed up at the Honor Roll, which had been brought out from the Main Hall and placed in a position of prominence on the platform. The gold star after Junior's name seemed brighter than the others. So many names, she thought; so many stars! And for a moment it all seemed a dream. Tomorrow they would go swimming in the pond. Billy would treat her to a frozen custard, and Junior would yank her pigtails . . .

And then it was time for the final roll call. The choir hummed the Alma Mater as the class filed up to receive their diplomas.

"Lucinda Anne Bishop—Honor Society, GAA, Latin Club, Class Sweetheart . . ."

Mr. Severence smiled warmly as he handed Lukie her diploma. And then, to her amazement, he took her hand and turned her around to face the audience.

"Less than half a grade point separated our top three scholars," he said. "This fine young lady is really the Class of Forty-four's third valedictorian."

The audience rose in applause.

"Congratulations, Lukie," Mr. Severence said. "Your school is very proud of you."

"Thank you, Mr. Severence," Lukie replied, her voice barely audible.

She hurried down from the platform, past the beaming faces of Miss Pray and Mr. Panella. And she was so deeply moved she started up the wrong aisle; Sally had to take her hand and lead her to her seat.

The ceremony drew to a close. The crowd stood with heads bowed as Mr. Schutze, the rector of St. Philip's, gave the benediction and offered a prayer for the invasion forces at Normandy. Lukie shut her eyes and thought of Billy in his P-47, screaming down over the German lines. Billy Butts of Zebron Falls. Who would have thought it?

"Rub your rabbit's foot, Billy," she murmured to herself. "Rub it hard and come back safe."

The band played the national anthem, and then Mr. Severence gave the closing announcements. There would be open-houses at the Pearsalls', the Bishops', and the Higbies'. Everyone was invited. A Navy recruiter would be at the post office on Monday, and job applications were being taken at the knitting mill.

"And, uh . . ." He fumbled in his pocket for a slip of paper. "Oh, yes—Mr. Knapp at the Sweet Shoppe wishes to announce free malts for the Class of Forty-four—but not all at one sitting, if you please."

A ripple of laughter ran through the crowd.

"And finally, if I may be permitted a word in behalf of the faculty. It is our job to help the young people of the community find their way. We hope that we have helped you and that you will think kindly of us."

Mr. Severence raised an arm in salute.

"Goodbye, good luck, come see us!"

There was a moment of silence, and then pandemonium broke loose. The band played. The choir sang. Graduation caps sailed into the air. And the fifty-six members of the Class of '44 let out a mighty roar. They had done it! They had run the course; they had made their mark.

"Oh, I just can't believe it's over!" Sally wailed.

There was much laughing and crying and horseplay. Plans for the future were discussed, pictures were exchanged, yearbooks were passed about for hurried inscriptions.

For several minutes the graduates made no effort to mingle with their families but, rather, stayed off by themselves, as if trying to prolong this final moment of unity, this bittersweet day that would never come again.

"Oh, Lukie!" Lorena Pearsall rushed up to Lukie in

tears. "We're moving to California!"

"California!" Lukie cried in dismay. "But . . ."

"My father's landed a job with an aircraft company. Oh, Lukie, we'll never see each other again!"

The girls embraced and clung to each other for a moment.

"Yes, we will, Lorena," Lukie said consolingly. "We'll hold reunions at the Saint James Hotel and sing songs in the tap room."

But she was remembering what her mother had said in the sunroom. Yes, it was time to let go. Their worlds were changing, and it was time to let go. But not entirely, for the Class of '44 would be a part of her forever, and the memories would be fresh and true and lovely.

"What about you, Lukie?" Lorena asked her. "Will you be staying in Zebron Falls?"

The sun had gone down. The air was cool and fragrant. Lights were coming on in the houses over on Wilcox Street. And in that moment, every sound, every smell of the soft spring evening made Lukie inexpressibly aware that she belonged to this town, this land, these people.

"I'll always stay here, Lorena," she said. "I'm a property owner."

She turned and started up the terraced lawn, to where her smiling family was waiting. Behind her, the choir was still singing.

"O Zebron Falls!"